The Sharson Chronicles

Beth Cortese

First published 2015
By Rowanvale Books Ltd
2nd Floor
220 High Street
Swansea
SA1 1NW
www.rowanvalebooks.com

A CIP catalogue record for this book is available from the British Library.
ISBN: 978-1-910607-67-1

Klanky's kidnapping

Cromdork lay awake on the floor of his study. Tired of researching nuclear power, he embarked on some healthy scheming instead. Since his comrade, Uglous, had been appointed King of Sharson, Cromdork had felt angry, as his friend had been severed from his side to take on a duty much more important. Cromdork protested passionately against this sudden appointment; in his opinion, Uglous was oblivious to the power at his very fingertips and he wouldn't be able to manage it. Uglous couldn't tackle a herd of bullies — how could he take on a responsibility as major as this?

After voicing his opinions and not receiving the desired result, Cromdork saw it as his duty as a friend — a very controlling friend — to offer to become Uglous' Royal Advisor. But Uglous had someone else in mind. This "someone" was Miss V.O.R.... no one knew her real name; before you ask, V.O.R. has nothing to do with shampoo. These initials stood for Voice of Reason; Uglous couldn't function without her. However, Miss V.O.R. had an obsessive hobby: shoe shopping. Cromdork was incredibly clever and resourceful, but also incredibly dominating and aggressive. Who would you choose: the sympathetic and genuine shoe-freak or the harsh control-freak? Cromdork was enraged when Uglous appointed Miss V.O.R. as chief advisor. He formulated a plan to prevent that *female* from becoming queen — with Uglous, any close female friend became more than a friend.

Cromdork searched far and wide, scanning the country for a weak queen. Finding a queen to allure and annoy Uglous at the same time was his goal; he needed to create a weak spot in Uglous' kingship. Cromdork had heard tales of the infamous Alaime Brane, whose name was symbolic as she was a rare specimen of stupidity. Cromdork found on meeting Alaime that she did indeed live up to her name and her reputation. He gave her a pair of large rectangular red glasses to wear, knowing that Uglous wouldn't be able to resist the "nerdy" look, no matter how much he wished to repel the girl.

As predicted, Uglous was drawn to Alaime's gawky glasses and romantic images of intellectual chats flashed through his idealistic mind. However, Alaime Brane didn't meet his expectations or the criteria on his ideal woman list. She was obnoxious, irritating and incredibly dim, which irritated the intelligent King. Cromdork had gone overboard with his "ideas" and now no longer cared for his friend's welfare - he just wanted that V.O.R. person to have as little power as possible. In his opinion, females like *her* shouldn't be in power; man was, and always had been, the superior race — such was his short-sighted and sexist state of mind. A limited and unfounded perspective, I'm sure you'll agree!

King Uglous knew that the only way to solve this disagreement was to send Cromdork away on a quest — that way the scientist could accomplish something and would forget his *ideas*. The following

Saturday Cromdork was banished from the kingdom until he could present an actual walking, talking alien. This reverse psychology was not Uglous' suggestion, but a joint one with Miss V.O.R. — they say behind every man there's a great woman.

***

Cromdork sat alone in his study, staring at Saturn and Uranus. Cromdork pondered subjects that others wouldn't. *Why is the grass green? How many nuclear bombs would it take to blow up the universe?* Everyone else was abnormal, he thought. Cromdork touched his black-hole bear lovingly. He knew that where he lived you didn't have to go far to come across an alien — the world was full of them.

His train of thought was interrupted by a knock on the study door; a soft, swift knock, a knock belonging to those of an airy, dozy and impatient disposition. This particular knock belonged to Herpursurly.

Cromdork looked up to see a curtain of purple splayed in front of him; the figure took up almost a quarter of the room. Shielding his eyes from the vibrant colour that encompassed Herpursurly and the ultra-violet rays seeping from it, Cromdork remembered when he first met her. That seemingly prehistoric week was the same week that Alaime was crowned Queen; Herpursurly was her 'arty' aunt and the only relative to attend her coronation.

Cromdork and Herpursurly had met at the coronation and realised that they had one thing in common; both desired revenge. Herpursurly's dog Klanky had been taken from her a year after he was born; he was to become one of the Knight's "steeds" as the King had discovered Klanky's record-breaking running abilities. Herpursurly was promised Klanky would be well cared for. She thought of Klanky every day and her aim was to win him back as soon as possible. As for Cromdork, he was power-hungry and wouldn't rest — this is true, he slept with his eyes open all those years — until his large derrière was upon the cushioned throne.

Herpursurly always wore gaudy shades of purple that could knock out any blind man. A doctor would probably diagnose Herpursurly with the purple plague! This obscure colour-scheme sickened Cromdork, he couldn't look at her or her artwork.

Cromdork thought her "work" was a "mess". Herpursurly was a lover of modern art. She would create using a paintbrush, makeup brush or an electric toothbrush — whatever was nearest to hand — and splatter it with paint. Cromdork was curious to see whether her "work" would sell, but Herpursurly said that would defeat its "spiritual purpose". Cromdork didn't have time for art and couldn't see its importance, which sickened Herpursurly.

Once, she attempted to explain "spiritual art" to Cromdork by saying, 'Art is a science.' Nothing excited Cromdork more than science. Science was something he could relate to; it made him daydream of chemical reactions, which always put a smile on his face!

Herpursurly arrived at the same time, every day, wearing the same violent shade of purple and the same blank expression before asking The Question.

'What do you want?' Cromdork growled, though he knew very well what she wanted.

'Have you thought of a plan yet?' Herpursurly asked impatiently.

'What do *you* think?' was the hostile response.

'I think that this place needs *brightening* up! Maybe…some purple?' Herpursurly gestured around the room; the latter statement was voiced innocently, childlike.

'NO PURPLE!' was Cromdork's explosive reply.

There was a long silence.

Finally, the purple persona filled the air with speech. 'I know!' she cried excitedly.

'You've thought of a plan?' Cromdork said, with mixture of hopefulness and doubt.

'No. But, I know a perfect shade of lilac that would complement your eyes,' Herpursurly said ecstatically.

Cromdork wasn't happy. He arched his almost non-existent eyebrows inwards and clenched his fists, but then thought better of it as Herpursurly raised a single eyebrow, her eyes interlocking with his in an unblinking stare.

***

Miss V.O.R. admired her sparkly toenails and pink heels by candlelight — the shoes were a gift from Uglous to thank her for the stress-ball she'd bought him. The stress-ball had been a hit; it released his anger, caused an insignificant amount of damage, but was strong enough to survive his iron grip. Miss V.O.R. had purchased Splat Sunder, a drowsy hedgehog, to act as Uglous' stress-ball. Uglous' tantrums made the hedgehog slightly less lazy; he got less sleep and lots of exercise, for when the King was angry — a frequent occurrence — he had to move incredibly quickly to avoid being splat asunder!

Miss V.O.R. glanced around the chamber; she noticed that the fruit bowl contained every type of fruit imaginable except, of course, for bananas. She sighed. This basic observation told Miss V.O.R. that Fidin Banas had had her evening meal already.

Fidin Banas was the second of the three royal advisors; she had an obsession with bananas which drove Uglous mad, as he detested them. She was a great confidante, people felt they could tell her all their worries — yet she was hardly ever around for them to do so, as she suffered from mind-boggling headaches. Perhaps this was due to the number of bananas she ate?

Uglous' third advisor was called Homan, and was also female. She was built like a bodyguard — no one knew how she came by the responsibility of advisor — and could single-handedly prop up eighteen articulated lorries whilst eating a baguette. After all, most women can do two things at once. Nothing prevented Homan from consuming food. Her solution to marital problems was to 'give your husband a good punch'... She was currently single.

Securing the elegant pink shoes onto her dainty feet and tying her hair up with a stripy ribbon, Miss V.O.R. retrieved Homan from the fridge and its contents. She then departed the chamber, sliding gently and expertly down the main banister with Homan about a metre behind. V.O.R. knew that it was a crime to be late for the Friday night feast and no one, especially not her, deserved to witness Uglous' vicious temper. A wave of relief passed through the courtiers in the banquet hall when they spied Miss V.O.R.

While the ravenous courtiers waited for King Uglous to arrive (they hadn't eaten that week, to build an appetite for twenty-six courses), two Jesters named Foolquin and Barthin entertained the guests. Foolquin was new to comedy. He was a diligent soul but unfortunately his sense of humour didn't match the courtiers'. It didn't surprise Foolquin that Homan was nowhere to be seen; she always seemed to have trouble getting past the banister without getting stuck, much to the jester's amusement.

He cleared his throat to address the hall. 'Homan? Where did you go, man? Oh dear! It seems on the main banister there is a traffic jam! Maybe she had too much ham!'

The courtiers were silent, causing Foolquin to blush. You'd have thought that after getting stuck on the banister for the fourteenth time, it would've at least been funny the first time. The beetroot-faced jester hid under his jingly hat.

It was Barthin's turn to attempt to amuse the critical courtiers. He removed the ridiculous red and yellow bell-infested hat and took a deep breath. He proudly switched on his hand-held computer and began to recite technological facts — his idea of entertainment. The crowd were amused by the enthusiasm in the jester's face and voice. Grins spread across the courtiers' faces and some laughed, mocking the jester and his bizarre passion for unreliable machines. Naïve Barthin now believed that he was their favourite jester, but Foolquin saw that, really, Barthin was the most mocked and felt sympathy for him. Poor Barthin!

Suddenly, the courtiers fell silent. Uglous entered the banquet hall carrying the dormant Splat Sunder — not a good omen — but the damage had already been done. Splat Sunder was curled tightly into a ball, his spikes pointing defensively outwards. Just as Uglous sat next to Miss V.O.R, a rugged-looking knight clanked forwards. However, the clanking sound didn't come from the knight, but from his noble steed, Klanky, a four-foot tall walnut-coloured dog, clad in a golden suit of armour. The knight was called Sir Ruddle. He and Klanky bowed low at Uglous' feet.

'Your Highness, I heard there was a situation on the stairs that needed handling,' the knight said.

'Yes, Sir Ruddle. I would be obliged if you could clear the stairs so we can get on with the banquet,' Uglous said, forcing a smile. The courtiers nodded in an agreement, their stomachs grumbling.

***

Back in Cromdork's study, Herpursurly was

making "art" by eating half a lemon and then splattering the rest of it with purple paint. Realising she had an abundant supply of the purple paint left, she deliberately covered herself in it to annoy Cromdork. Notorious villains are no fun, especially if all they talk about is physics. Her face fell when she noticed that Cromdork hadn't torn up the study curtains in rage at the sight of her, purple and dripping. She stood there, her eyes wide with anticipation. Eventually Cromdork showed signs of intelligent life and smiled —— like a crocodile who'd swallowed a gob-smacked dentist. For the first time in five years, Herpursurly blinked, before swallowing the purple lump in her throat.

'Herpursurly, sit down on that pile of newspapers while the paint dries. I have a plan.'

Herpursurly squelched across to the pile of newspapers. 'You do?' she recovered her voice.

'Yes. I hope you're hungry — we're going to a banquet!' Cromdork threw a book entitled *Uranus* to the artist, who appeared interested in the pictures inside.

***

Meanwhile on the castle banister, Boasty Bower was in a hurry to get to the banquet. She had been looking at Glitzy Shoes Online, a site recommended to her by Miss V.O.R. Once she'd started shopping, she couldn't stop. It had made her late and now she suffered, starving behind a weeping blob stuck in front of her.

'Look, aren't you hungry?' Boasty Bower said in frustration.

'Ye-es, but… I'm…stuck!' Homan sniffled hysterically.

'You didn't eat before you came out, did you?' Boasty questioned sympathetically.

'Only a few tubs of Haagen Daaz,' Homan replied pathetically.

'Ok. Well, maybe we can ease you forward a bit?' Boasty said, trying to sound kind.

'It's no use! I'm scared that if I shift forward, I'll ruin my face — I just had it lifted,' Homan replied.

'Oh.' Boasty Bower was lost for words. Homan stared at her expectantly. 'I mean, it looks great, you can't even tell you've had it done!' Boasty added hurriedly. She then muttered to herself, 'I wish I'd had something to eat before I came out, but I just *had* to look at those pink stilettos, I *had* to! Why does such a predicament always befall people like me when no one's around to help?'

No sooner had Boasty said this when Sir Ruddle appeared with Klanky trotting proudly behind.

'We're stuck!' Boasty cried.

'And I'm hungry!' Homan yelled.

'Right. Firstly, Homan?' Sir Ruddle began.

'What?' Homan rudely replied.

'I heard from a certain Voice of Reason that you've been eating Haagen Daaz recently,' Sir Ruddle continued, unfazed.

'I haven't!' Homan protested.

'You don't happen to have any left on your fingers or a spare tub lying around, do you?' Sir Ruddle continued, the cogs in his chivalrous mind turning quickly. Homan sheepishly presented a travel-size tub of ice-cream.

'Brilliant! It's still cold!' Sir Ruddle exclaimed jovially.

'Don't eat it!' Homan screeched.

'I've no intention of doing so,' the selfless Knight responded. 'I'm going to rub it on the banister.'

'But that'll take the polish off!' Boasty interjected, a lover of polished surfaces.

'Do you or don't you want to be rescued? This is an exclusive service, don't you know?' Sir Ruddle said defensively.

'Just do it!' Homan shouted, reaching seven on the Richter scale.

Sir Ruddle rubbed the contents of the tub on the banister, licking the Belgian chocolate flavour off his armour at intervals.

'Ok, ladies. Klanky will slide from the top of the banister, giving us some force to move Miss Bower along —'

'You know my name?!' Boasty interrupted.

'Yes, I have a list of all the damsels that are likely to be in distress,' he blushed, before continuing. 'I will be at the bottom to catch you both and the Haagen Daaz ice-cream should gently slide Homan along, got it?'

'Ingenious!' Boasty exclaimed — which was unusual, as she didn't dish out compliments easily.

Klanky clanked down the banister, gaining speed as he rolled like a sausage dog. He hit Boasty, who began to tumble down the banister towards Homan. Slowly, Homan clenched her facial muscles and eased herself down. When she got close to the end she gave up and sat there huffing and puffing, until Boasty and Klanky came rolling towards her. Boasty and Klanky gave her the last push she needed and they all landed in a heap on Sir Ruddle's boots. Well, all except Homan, who was precariously balanced in Sir Ruddle's arms, yelping in terror. She grabbed the knight's shoulders, clinging on for dear life, clutching her tub of Haagen Daaz. Unable to support Homan and her precious tub, Sir Ruddle collapsed. Klanky was proud of their triumph and barked happily, licking Boasty Bower's face. Usually Boasty would've objected to the unhygienic creature climbing over her, but she was pretty impressed by the knight and his "noble-steed".

So, on the back of Klanky, Sir Ruddle and Boasty Bower were welcomed into the banquet hall by a sea of cheers with Homan trudging behind. Homan hid the tub of Haagen Daaz under her robe when she noticed Uglous watching her.

'Well done, Sir Ruddle!' Uglous smiled and patted Klanky's shaggy head.

Suddenly, the doors of the hall were flung open. Light flooded in — ultra-violet light

— revealing the outline of a familiar man, slightly hunched and grey-haired despite his youthful age. Cowering behind the hunched figure was a... Well, Uglous didn't quite know what it was. It didn't resemblance anything he'd seen before. Maybe Cromdork had fulfilled his task? The tension in the court couldn't have been cut, not even with a chainsaw, but was momentarily postponed by a demanding voice;

'I'm NOT LATE! Well excuse me, Mr Blingin Sheep!'

'Now, now, Alaime, don't make a scene,' Alaime's stylist, the Blingin Sheep, said coolly.

'*I'm* not making a *scene*. You were the one who took so long styling my hair. *So* it's *your* fault,' Alaime said.

'You cannot rush art! Besides,' the Blingin Sheep snapped, 'if you remember correctly, you were late to start off with, because you couldn't find your lip-gloss when you knew I had some spare anyway. Touché, Alaime.'

'Hmmph!' was Alaime's response.

Herpursurly watched with interest. She found it truly amazing to see the way the sheep had transformed her niece. However, it didn't take a brain surgeon to realise that no matter how intelligent Alaime was made to look, no amount of nerdy glasses could hide her lack of intellect. Many of the courtiers put Alaime's dimness down to 'being blonde', but this simply wasn't true. Alaime used this as an excuse, even when she dyed her hair a different shade! Herpursurly realised why the Blingin Sheep was named so. He had a huge diamante and gold earring in one ear and a large, rectangular medallion around his neck. As he spoke and gesticulated using his hands, all the rings on his fingers jingled. Herpursurly was mightily impressed.

She was jolted out of her trance by Cromdork's voice.

'Let's go, remember the plan!' he snarled.

She rolled her eyes up into her purple eyelids and followed Cromdork as he approached Uglous and Alaime. Alaime looked down on them from her throne. She knew that there was a history of friction between Cromdork and her husband, and she loved fights. She crossed her fingers behind her back, wishing one would break out. To her, either one's injury would be no loss as she disliked both of them. The only person she really cared for was herself.

'Cromdork, you're...back?' Uglous

stammered.

'Yes, *Your Highness,*' Cromdork replied smugly. 'I brought you the alien you required.'

'Ah,' Uglous leaned forward as Cromdork brought Herpursurly forward. 'Purple?' Uglous questioned, squinting at Herpursurly's complexion.

Herpursurly couldn't contain herself. 'Yes. What's *wrong* with purple? You know, that's quite offensive, anyone would think you are racist.'

The courtiers gasped at this accusation. They looked from Herpursuly to Uglous and back to Herpursurly again.

'I'm sorry. I didn't know you understood what we were saying, being an alien,' Uglous said, in an attempt to recover himself.

'So you're saying I'm stupid now?' Herpursurly replied aggressively — a behaviour copied from Cromdork.

Alaime felt like joining in to provoke a real punch-up but thought better of it, as it would only backfire on her.

Uglous blushed beetroot as compliments fell from his lips. 'No! I didn't mean that! You've a lovely complexion and have travelled far, which takes knowledge of geography. Where are you from?'

'Uranus,' she replied.

Foolquin grinned and began to voice a well-rehearsed joke to Uglous, who quickly silenced him.

'Really? Well, that explains the purple,' Uglous replied with interest.

'Yes, the royal planet, the "*purpley*" planet,' Herpursurly stressed, giving Uglous a sly grin she had learnt from watching Cromdork practising his in the mirror. Uglous turned away from Herpursurly; he was afraid of flirting with an alien, especially one that didn't blink.

'Well… Welcome back!' Uglous said in a friendly voice. However, inside he felt very nervous about Cromdork's return.

The courtiers cheered, believing the two rivals were at peace. They weren't. As always, Cromdork had more slimy schemes up his sleeve.

'Cromdork, would it be alright to ask your "alien" guest to work at our windmill, The Royal Draftness? We really need helping hands, no matter what colour they are,' Uglous added tactfully.

Cromdork didn't care. Like Alaime, he was self-seeking and he didn't need

Herpursurly for his next scheme.

'Yes. In fact, I'm sure she'd be willing to work long hour shifts for *you*,' Cromdork said cunningly. He knew that Uglous would be keen to make Herpursurly work constantly; Uglous loved to make sure diligent workers had enough work to keep them interested. Cromdork then lowered his voice and added for good measure, 'Workaholics, these Uranians.'

'Then it's agreed!' Uglous smiled at Herpursurly, who hadn't been paying attention to anything that had been said; she'd been too busy watching the Blingin Sheep devour a grass salad with golden sprinkles. That explained her shock at being led to a grand white windmill with grey propellers in the shape of baseball caps.

Herpursurly was informed that the windmill had a terrible habit of roaming around the countryside, swinging itself from side to side, whistling and hitting things in its wake. She was advised to remain with the windmill, wherever it was. The name of the windmill was The Royal Draftness, for Miss V.O.R. had insisted that everything in the grounds be given a name to give it a sense of purpose. The Royal Draftness was an appropriate name for the windmill, who was flatulent and created his own wind. Cromdork had insisted the windmill be given tablets for its wind. After a time the wind built up, which was extremely unpleasant for the kingdom when The Royal Draftness forgot to take his tablets and "let rip". After that, Cromdork was overruled by the advisors and courtiers — besides, without the tablets, he was energy efficient. The kingdom's source of wind power would never run out as long as baked beans were still available.

It was early evening and Herpursurly had ideas. After two hours of solid work on the windmill, she was sick of the white paint that covered The Royal Draftness. Purple would make the windmill look a lot bolder and lilac propellers would complement the purple. The Royal Draftness was irritated by her plans to re-decorate his exterior, as purple didn't match his reputation and his sideways walk. Herpursurly's anger re-emerged when she saw Sir Ruddle riding on *her* Klanky. He was *her* dog! She no longer had any interest in Cromdork's plan; she only had eyes for Klanky — and the Blingin Sheep! She decided that before she made her departure she would have both of them! Cackling, she departed in search of a paintbrush.

***

A new day dawned on the kingdom. The Royal Draftness had had a rough night; he had attended a party (he was finding it hard to remember things) and was "swung-over". There had been flapping skirts, mouldy cheeses and scotch eggs. Then chillies, mushy peas, beans and, of course, curry sauce. And now, as always, he felt the effects.

It was eight o'clock in the morning, and Splat Sunder was awake. He no longer felt the need to curl up, he was a new hedgehog! Uglous had been very pleasant to him — Miss V.O.R's presence had benefited the whole kingdom. These happy thoughts were knocked out of the poor hedgehog's skull as both he and the rest of the kingdom received a rude awakening; there was an ear-splitting explosion, followed by a long, low-pitched rumble. Cromdork was surprised that the methane coming out of the flatulent windmill didn't blow the kingdom away or suffocate everyone in the process. The Royal Draftness grinned, showing off immaculate white teeth. He felt truly relieved. He was also impressed with himself — he had topped his last record! Splat's spikes shot up and he curled back into a ball, safe from the world once more.

Sir Ruddle and Klanky jumped out of their skins on hearing the disgusting noise. They heard cries of, 'Urrgh! Smells like rotten egg and stilton!' Rushing to action, they grabbed bottles of perfume and air-freshener — Boasty was particularly helpful with supplying perfume and Homan had cans of long-lasting air freshener.

Off they rode, equipped with perfume, air-freshener and a cork, towards The Royal Draftness. Concerned for Sir Ruddle's safety, Boasty — wearing her baby pink dressing-gown — rode after the dynamic duo. It wasn't long before the toxic aroma was eradicated using all the perfume, sprays, air-fresheners and aerosols in the kingdom. Sir Ruddle and Boasty were concerned about preventing the stench from spreading further. They rammed a sturdy-looking cork into…let's call it The Royal Draftness' exhaust. Then they cautioned the windmill not to consume foods that'd make him "over-draughty".

However, one difficulty remained;

Herpursurly was trapped inside the windmill.

Klanky, wearing a gas mask, rushed inside the windmill to rescue the "alien". He scanned the room, trying to locate Herpursurly. She'd already seen Klanky through a crack in the door. With a rope, she lassoed the poor mutt and dragged him out through a secret entrance, escaping with the kidnapped Klanky.

***

Another scheming female had also carried out a theft. Alaime Brane was tired of married life and the lack of punch-ups. She'd had her eye on a rich physician for a long time and they'd decided to "elope". They weren't engaged, but Alaime could be persuasive — and even pleasant — when in the mood. Alaime slid down the castle banister, heading towards the stables. Earlier, Boasty had taken Alaime's favourite mare, so she scanned each stall and chose a ginger horse on which she could ride in style. Alaime didn't look upon this as stealing. After all, she'd been married to Uglous for quite some time so what he owned was, technically, hers.

***

Boasty Bower and Sir Ruddle waited patiently for Klanky to emerge from The Royal Draftness. As they waited, the windmill swayed and rapped to a fast beat. His rhymes were associated with "bling" and "fast food".

The windmill stopped rapping. 'Who you waitin' for, bro?'

'My noble steed,' the knight replied.

'Huh?' The Royal Draftness murmured.

'Klanky, the big dog. You know, the one that clanks as he walks? Klanky,' the knight said slowly, making sure the windmill understood.

'Oh yeah! The one that left wiv the broad. Didn't seem ter be noble at all, man,' was the dislocated response.

'There must be some mistake. Not my Klanky! We're a team!' Sir Ruddle whined.

'No mistake. But if it makes yer feel better, the dog didn't seem too ecstatic 'bout it,' the Royal Draftness finished nonchalantly.

'I'm sure we'll find him,' Boasty added warmly. 'You're a noble knight and, like you said, you're a team — Klanky won't be able to function without you.'

Sir Ruddle was consoled. He turned to face Boasty. 'You're right. For now on, *you*, my dear, will be my partner in chivalry.'

Boasty blushed; she felt honoured to help Sir Ruddle on his quest. 'Well, Sir. Do you have any idea who would steal Klanky? I don't think the windmill is going to be very helpful on the matter.'

'I have my suspicions,' Sir Ruddle replied. 'Let us go, mistress! We will ride upon your noble steed.'

Boasty blushed even more deeply at being called his mistress. Their quest had begun.

***

King Uglous was informed of Klanky's disappearance and of Sir Ruddle's and Boasty's quest to find him. Whilst knight and maiden searched the kingdom, Uglous and Miss V.O.R. looked for the walnut-coloured dog within the castle.

'He can't have gone far, especially if he was dragged against his own will,' Miss V.O.R. said knowingly.

Klanky's kidnapping was the perfect distraction; it enabled Cromdork to catch everyone off-guard with his plan. No one could stop him now. Not even the Voice of Reason; her concern for others was her downfall. Females, Cromdork thought, were too sentimental. He didn't feel remorse for the mangy mutt; it was an animal, and humans — in his opinion — were superior. Of course, he knew who the dog-napper was — not that he cared. It was obvious as Herpursurly was off the scene. The dog-napper's distraction left him free to conjure up a treacherous plan! Everything was in his favour today.

As you may have guessed, Cromdork was after the throne, having been banished from the kingdom. Like most villains, he wanted revenge and power. However, Cromdork wasn't the average 'mad scientist'; he knew that the throne couldn't be taken by force. He would have to win the courtiers over. He needed a makeover, fast, and he knew who could help him.

***

On the outskirts of the kingdom, a campfire blazed. Klanky and Herpursurly sat either side of the fire.

'Do you remember me?' she asked Klanky earnestly.

'No,' the perplexed animal replied.

'I am — was — your owner. You were very young when I looked after you,' she said, gazing down at her purple toe-nails.

'You must be the "Purple Lady", the one who covers everything in paint?' he said.

'That's me,' Herpursurly said quietly.

'I don't remember you, but my brother mentioned you often.'

'Really?!' Herpursurly squealed.

'He always was a fan of your artwork,' Klanky said gently. He'd begun to notice his kidnapper wasn't that bad after all.

'We used to finger-paint together — or paw-print, in his case,' she smiled.

'Where are we going, exactly?' Klanky said, changing the subject.

'Don't you want to go back?' she replied, confused.

'Yes, but you're not that bad for a villain. Why did you bring me here, out of all the places in the kingdom?' Klanky asked, surveying the forest they were in.

'Well…' she began, closing her eyes and remembering.

***

Back at Sharson castle, the Blingin Sheep was awake. He rose early every morning to clean his rings and earrings and, of course, the crown jewels, kept under his protection. No one talked to him much, but he and the windmill had been firm friends at one stage. That was before the Blingin Sheep had been promoted from grazing in the castle grounds to Royal Stylist and The Royal Draftness had remained in the lowly position of Royal Windmill.

He was engrossed in his work, carefully examining every inch of the gold, when there was a knock at the door. The sheep rose to his hooves gingerly and left the jewellery on his desk, winking at him. He turned the door knob languidly, revealing a hunched figure with hair slicked back and a demonic smile across his lips. The sheep stylist flinched at this sight, before showing his visitor to a vacant chair and closing the door silently. Although the visitor's gaze was transfixed on the door, his eyes moved around their sockets shiftily. Despite being taken by surprise, the Blingin Sheep demonstrated an aura of ease.

'Can I help you, sir?' he asked courteously.

'I need a makeover — and fast.' Cromdork

lowered his voice, adding a sense of urgency to his request.

'I can see that!' the sheep replied abruptly.

'I want you to teach me to be...' Cromdork said a little nervously.

'Hmm?' the Blingin Sheep murmured.

'Well...'

'Go on,' the stylist said impatiently.

'Hip. A cool dude,' Cromdork replied.

The Blingin Sheep bleated, stifling a grin. '*That* will cost you,' he said, returning to his business-like manner.

'I've no desire to pay you,' Cromdork said bluntly.

'I'm afraid I cannot help you.'

'I have another offer.'

'Tell me quickly. I've wasted enough time talking,' the sheep said.

'Do this for me, and I'll see to it that Uglous is off the throne.'

There was a long pause as the stylist stroked his bearded chin, contemplating Cromdork's offer.

'I'll take it,' was the decisive reply.

'No questions asked?' Cromdork sneered. The stylist shook his head. 'Good! We start tomorrow.' The scheming scientist was over the moon and stood up to leave.

'Let's start today,' the Blingin Sheep said.

It was Cromdork's turn to be surprised.

The sheep smirked at the villain's amazement. 'I love a challenge.'

Herpursurly would've been enraged by the alliance between Cromdork and the Royal Stylist but luckily fate had laid out a new road for her, one which led away from Cromdork.

***

Far from the Sharson throne, Sir Ruddle and Boasty were tired from riding across the countryside. They dismounted and began to look around them when they spotted the unmistakeable figure of Klanky. The armoured dog was chasing an apple — a purple apple.

'Klanky!' Sir Ruddle yelled. 'You're safe!'

Klanky and Sir Ruddle shared a manly embrace before dusting their armour off. Their faces were luminous with joy.

Boasty secured her horse to a nearby tree and located Herpursurly, who was staring at the ground shyly. The "alien" now felt guilty about what she'd done. Boasty understood this and approached her.

'Why would an alien steal a four foot dog?'

'He used to be mine when he was a puppy. And I'm *not* an alien, it's just purple paint,' Herpursurly said sadly.

'Right…' Boasty replied doubtfully.

'I'm really sorry,' Herpursurly said humbly.

'Tell Sir Ruddle that — he's over there.'

'Can't you?' Herpursurly said timidly.

'If you really are sorry, you'll tell him yourself,' Boasty said moodily.

Herpursurly apologised to Boasty for a second time and then to Sir Ruddle. She explained her new plan to search for Klanky's brother, who was in need of an owner.

'Good for you,' Sir Ruddle exclaimed. 'We'd come with you, but we have to get back to Uglous.'

'Take this.' Boasty handed Herpursurly a style magazine to encourage her to rethink her "purple look." She was thrilled.

After a meal of purple apples — the painted skin was removed before consumption — the three travelled to the castle with a light breeze behind them.

***

Cromdork was pleased with the results of his makeover. That sheep really knew his stuff! That was an art, even more so than science, Cromdork thought. The makeover had been an enlightening experience for him.

The new Cromdork had a hoop earring on one ear, curly long brown hair with no grey patches — it had been dyed — rosy cheeks, black leather boots and a leather jacket to match his tight, black trousers. Observers would have described him as looking very "in" and "with it".

Cromdork entered the banquet hall considerably less hunched. Totally unrecognisable, he addressed the courtiers.

'What's up?' Cromdork said.

The courtiers stared at him blankly. Then a single female voice called out, 'Oooh…he's gorrrgeousss! I do love a bit of eyeliner on a man!'

Cromdork grinned, his teeth now pearly white — dentistry had come a long way, thanks to science, of course!

'Thank you, thank you. Peace y'all! That's what I'm gonna give ya — peace! Put me on the throne!' Cromdork bellowed, blowing kisses to all.

The kingdom's response was quite extraordinary. Women and children stood on the tables and clapped. Cromdork was confident that nobody could stop him now, and he was right— for now.

***

Inside one of the castle chambers, Uglous peered out the window; he spied a black and white clad figure below, charming the crowd. Something about the figure seemed familiar, as though he knew him. Hold on, he *did* know him — it was Cromdork. An improved Cromdork, but still a sneering, manipulative science geek! Uglous was distraught. The Blingin Sheep must have done this; no one else could've created such a fashionable man! Where was the chivalry? Sir Ruddle wasn't back, and what of Klanky? Miss V.O.R. had given up on looking for them, which meant she was probably out shopping. What was he to do? He banged his head against the window, hoping everything would go away. Uglous spied Splat Sunder and grabbed him. He chucked the hedgehog down the main banister, watching the poor thing bounce off the walls, then threw his head into his hands and waited for a saviour.

Back in the banquet hall, a saviour had arrived loaded with shopping bags. Miss V.O.R. rummaged through the bags looking for a particular bar of chocolate to share with the courtiers to celebrate Klanky's homecoming. She made her way through the forest of legs and arms in confusion. When she reached the front of the crowd she noticed that Cromdork, not Uglous, was sitting on the throne. It may have been a trendier Cromdork, but it was still the same man. Miss V.O.R. could tell he was evil by the ugly leather boots he was wearing — shoes were very important! As soon as she made this vital observation she power-walked over to Cromdork and raised her voice above the jabbering courtiers.

'*Your Highness,*' she began sarcastically. 'What's more important to you, the welfare of your kingdom or scientific research?'

Accidentally lapsing into his old ways, Cromdork replied, 'Science of course!' He cursed under his breath as the words left his tongue.

'My friends, this is no monarch, but our very own Cromdork: black-hearted and science-obsessed,' Miss V.O.R. concluded.

The crowd booed at the angry and embarrassed Cromdork as he ran, heading towards the Royal Draftness' latest "hang-out".

Now certain that Cromdork had left the kingdom, Miss V.O.R. disappeared out into the corridor that led to the main banister where she found Uglous. He was shaking. She took him by the arm and led him into the hall. They were welcomed back by whistles and cheers from the courtiers. Uglous and Miss V.O.R. ascended the throne, bowing and curtseying, where the crown was once again placed on Uglous' head. It was a joyous occasion and the peak of happiness rose even higher when Klanky clanked in. The noble steed was closely followed by Miss Boasty Bower and Sir Ruddle, and the pair had an announcement to make.

'Friends! Miss Bower and I are to be married on the 'morrow!' Sir Ruddle said happily.

Toasts were made, followed by savoury treats and grand desserts. The whole kingdom celebrated and V.O.R. was crowned queen. As for Splat Sunder, he was free to retire as Uglous was much calmer with Miss V.O.R. as his queen. The Fools researched their jokes and, from that day on, worked in the court for many years, becoming funnier and more popular.

Homan went on a diet and took up polo in the castle grounds. Fidin Banas was employed as Royal Cook — her speciality was banana delicacies. The pesky Alaime Brane was last seen in a stable outside the kingdom with Boasty's horse. She paid for her crime by dealing with unpleasant smelling stables, which she was now qualified to muck out.

Herpursurly found Klanky's brother and became his rightful owner. She was also the first breeder of purple poodles. This made people more appreciative of the colour purple, eventually.

Cromdork, the Blingin Sheep and The Royal Draftness escaped, leaving no trace of their whereabouts. Rumour had it that they opened a travelling hairdressers together, entitled "Hair today, gone tomorrow". Cromdork received 70% of the profits as Manager, and the Blingin Sheep was Chief Hair Stylist and Cutter, of course. And The Royal Draftness? He was plied with dozens of air-fresheners and made a very useful hairdryer!

Loopy Lou and the Amazing Tulip

Our story begins with the Amazing Tulip, who was petals-over-stem in love with Mr J. Long Flagpole. The Amazing Tulip was a well-known resident of Arbsitchy; a tulip with a rare aroma, she gave out amazing advice to passing travellers. Mr J. Long Flagpole was also a respected resident in the village. His occupation was to welcome those visiting the village and, as Arbsitchy's tallest resident, there was no one better to stand on top of the hill waving their flag.

When an old, spotty witch named Loopy Lou heard of the Amazing Tulip's success and Mr J. Long Flagpole's love for her, she was jealous — literally green with envy —

which made her warts and spots worse! Her desire was to wrap her razor-sharp fingernails around the dashing Mr J. Long Flagpole. Feeling frustrated, she called upon her old friends; False Lashes, Captain Black-Eye and Spam Insane.

Spam Insane, one of her main supporters, always trailed after her and obeyed her orders. He was a mucky peasant that nobody wanted to hire because of his ferocity and his insatiable appetite. False Lashes was a superficial female with 'attitude' and dead straight fake eyelashes. Lastly, Captain Black-Eye was a drunken fighter who bruised easily. Loopy Lou's ambition was to quench the thirst and hunger of Spam (who clearly was insane, probably because he worked for her) by feeding him the sweet sap of our dear Amazing Tulip. This was a cruel and wicked scheme that False Lashes and Captain Black-Eye would be part of too.

If you're at home reading this, I suggest you raid your cupboards or fridges now as the next part is where the baddies come in; you'll need sustenance to keep up with the action!

Using her sharpened fingernails, Loopy Lou dug a long tunnel, huffing and cursing as she reached the top of Arbsitchy Hill. A normal being would lack strength, but not Loopy Lou. She followed a strict diet of calcium, spinach and McDonalds, the first two improving her bone and muscle structure and the latter... Who knows? It certainly didn't improve the pus content in her pores! With a loud battle-cry, Loopy Lou reached the surface of the soil, recharging her black magic, before rising from the tunnel and dragging Mr J. Long Flagpole back down with her. Her logic was that nobody would ever think of looking for a seven-foot long flagpole below the surface. With a toothy grin, she sealed the tunnel with thorny lashes (donated by False Lashes) and ordered Captain Black-Eye to stand guard with False Lashes.

Most villainous plans take years to prepare and are costly, but Loopy Lou's schemes were effective as she knew people who were desperate for work. The principle was easy. All she had to do was separate the two "lovers" from each other. As False Lashes and Captain Black-Eye preferred to work as a team, Lou left the rest to Spam Insane.

The Amazing Tulip had been told to

meet her aunt for tea in a nearby overgrown forest — which, of course, was a setup; she was soon to be ambushed (or rather, 'Spam-bushed'). Spam Insane anticipated her arrival and had only eaten a light snack that day. He smacked his chops together as the sun set.

Luckily, the inquisitive frogs of The Sloan Ranger - the village sheriff and friend of The Amazing Tulip - had heard of Loopy Lou's schemes. They instantly hopped off the local lily pad down to the Sloan Ranger's "pad". The Sloan Ranger was furious when she heard Loopy Lou's latest scheme.

She marched down to the witch's grotty house to voice an outburst that she'd suppressed for years. 'LOU! Listen to me, you vile, volcanic freak!' The Sloan Ranger's words echoed around the farmyard.

'Yeah chicken? And your little webbed-footed weasels?' The reply was a congested snarl.

'They are frogs!' the Sloan Ranger retorted.

'Whatever, chicken!' Lou snarled.

'I've told you already, they're frogs. Now to the point. Firstly, you need a healthier diet and some Clearasil. Secondly, there's no point in holding Mr J. Long Flagpole hostage and forcing him to marry you — he doesn't love you.'

The Sloan Ranger decided that now wasn't the time to dwell on the damage of her words, later would be more appropriate, possibly over a cup of tea with some friends. Now was the time to take a step back, or five, from the situation.

Five seconds was the time it took for Loopy Lou to process this — enough time for The Sloan Ranger to take cover. Lou's first impulse was to send hate-mail contained in magical envelopes, bringing sorrow to all, but she needed a less time-consuming course of action. Hopping on her broomstick, she flew around like a headless chicken, screaming all the way, her nails denting the wood until she reached the tunnel she dug earlier. Her eyes watered as she thought about all the horrible insults directed at her, but instead of watery tears, she cried streams of lava, like a volcano. The flow was so great that it knocked Captain Black-Eye sideways and frizzled his beard. He crashed into a wall, bruising his limbs. The spiky lashes at the entrance of the tunnel curled inwards, before springing outwards and catapulting

False Lashes downhill.

The heroic Mr J. Long Flagpole ran as fast as his lanky legs would carry him, waving the Arbsitchy flag as he bounded to the Amazing Tulip's rescue. Spam Insane held her tightly in his iron-like fist. Using his quick thinking, Mr Long J. Flagpole pulled out a half-eaten packet of Starbursts and threw them into Spam Insane's open mouth.

Spam felt a surge of sour fruits; the taste was like nothing he'd ever experienced. He felt satisfied. To show his appreciation, he released a huge belch towards the astonished Loopy Lou. The stench was so strong that the spots on her face exploded and, because most of her was made up of pus, she exploded.

Peace was restored. Spam's appetite was satisfied with Starbursts. The Sloan Ranger had helped a friend and released an outburst she'd concealed for far too long. The Amazing Tulip and Mr J. Long Flagpole got engaged. And guess what? They lived happily-ever-after in Arbsitchy.

Rayra and Breezy: A tale of flirtatious fleas and greasy sheep

Rayra was a fierce tigress, though in size she was hardly daunting. She could be as sweet and cuddly as a spring lamb but, when provoked, her mood would turn into a stormy sea, miles away from a lighthouse.

Her accomplice was a beanpole called Breezy, who was calm and sunny and helped to guide Rayra through all sorts of problematic places. Soon it would be Rayra's turn to help Breezy.

In this story, both face a forest full of intimidating trees, foreign, flirtatious fleas and tasteless greasy sheep. As you can imagine, all of these factors strengthened their friendship.

Rayra had visited lands filled with various species, some similar to herself and Breezy. This land was different. Not only were the inhabitants spirited males, but they were from a totally different culture to the two companions. A riotous clan, they were unused to females and new creatures. Oblivious and unprepared, Rayra entered the dense forest - strong-willed and effervescent – alongside Breezy, who was equipped with an insulated scarf.

Dusk fell upon the travellers; full of fatigue, they halted in front of a large tree. The tree dominated the whole forest, its branches reaching up to the sky in a nonchalant shrug. The mesmerised travellers' trance was interrupted by a distant cry. Rayra sharpened her claws, alarmed by the eerie sound. Breezy, however, skipped forward, searching for the culprit. All was quiet. Another cry was heard, then several cries, which became a chorus.

Rayra looked wildly about her and, seeing nothing, felt frustrated. She wondered why Breezy was giggling hysterically, and then noticed a herd of fleas clambering over

Breezy's insulated scarf. They sang extremely badly whilst playing air-instruments and tickling Breezy! Then the frisky fleas jumped onto Rayra's back. Dazed and confused, she didn't bother to snap at them, mainly because — and this was a secret which only Breezy knew — she'd recently become a vegetarian. Her new diet included vast amounts of sunflower seeds and carrots. Even though the fleas didn't know this, they bravely scurried around and play-fought on the tigress' back. Rayra was amazed at their bravery; no creature had ever *dared* to do so before.

Breezy's hysteria, Rayra's disconcertion and the behaviour of the raucous fleas ceased at the sound of a deep and resonant voice, quite unlike the squeaky jabbering of the fleas.

'Cool it, you philandering rascals! Scoffin's here now, you ladies need not fear,' the voice rumbled.

Rayra blushed as she admired the unique button-nose that the chief flea, Scoffin, possessed. It was love at first sniff; Rayra's aroma was unlike any Scoffin had smelt before, for the sweet scent of watermelon lifted his hairy legs into the air with joy.

Sensing a passionate atmosphere between Rayra and Scoffin, the tactful Breezy suggested that they play "Hide and Seek" to get to know each other better, knowing full well that this was a perfect opportunity for Rayra to show off her skills in the art of camouflage. Within moments, all the fleas had disappeared except for Scoffin, who was supposedly helping Rayra "count". Breezy had to find somewhere to hide and she knew those funny little fleas would have an effortless task losing themselves in the undergrowth. But she, a beanpole, was so obvious, her lanky legs and knobbly knees stuck out all over the place. She would have to give her position a fast but thorough bit of thought.

On hearing Scoffin's voice, Breezy gripped the end of her insulated scarf and, using her initiative, lassoed a high and sturdy-looking branch of the elegant, central tree. She pulled herself up, finding footholds along the way. She almost fell in her rush to secure herself fully in the tree. However, Breezy clung tightly to her scarf and landed uncomfortably, yet safely, in the grand structure, with her legs poking out of the top. What would you do with a pair of thighs that went on forever? Although the most noticeable tree in the forest was now even more eye-catching with a pair of scraggly legs and knobbly knees waving on top of it, the birds overhead took no notice, regarding it as an unfortunate piece of greenery that had been given too much fertiliser, causing a deformed spurt of energetic and oversized leaves.

Roadrunner, the Albatross of Mystery, was intrigued by this unusual sight. He had a tedious lifestyle and whenever something the least bit exciting cropped up — literally, in this case — he'd investigate it, before running away swiftly. His tendency to run away explained the name Roadrunner – but what about the title "Albatross of Mystery"? Well, the reason why he ran away from everything was the real mystery! For Roadrunner, this was an opportunity not to be missed. Dramatically diving low, he crash-landed on top of Breezy, who fell heels over head into a patch of rotting cherries; this added to her sticky situation, but at least she was the right way up.

Having an albatross on your stomach isn't a particularly nice experience, especially if they've been eating fish! Roadrunner dusted his feathers off and stared at the incredibly long and partly dismantled Breezy, full of curiosity.

Reawakened by the reviving, yet revolting, stench of fish, Breezy opened her eyes. Seeing Breezy's sapphire eyes filled Roadrunner with more curiosity — what could be in them to make them so captivating? Then he remembered his personal philosophy: 'Curiosity killed the cat, but lingering and pursuing one's feelings confuses an albatross for life.'

Roadrunner decided that was all the excitement he could muster. He forgot all about Breezy's sapphire eyes and before poor Breezy could utter a gasp of surprise, the creature vanished. She was flabbergasted and perplexed by the lack of explanation of the creature's sudden arrival and disappearance.

Vaguely disorientated and with a slight headache, Breezy gave the remainder of her energy to Rayra, listening with full attention to the tigress' animated talk of her day with Scoffin. She filled Breezy in on every detail of "Hide and Seek" that Breezy had missed since her fall, and how the fleas had been impressed with Rayra's skill at turning herself invisible. This talk of invisibility made

Breezy remember the strange bird whom she'd met earlier that day. She recollected the smell of rotting cherries and the stench of fish and told her tale to Rayra.

'Have another carrot, sweetie,' the tigress said, smiling. 'I think your eyesight's beginning to fail, because *I* never saw a bird of that description!' This exclamation was kindly meant in Rayra's "lamb-mode".

'I'm serious,' Breezy whispered, 'it just… disappeared,' she sighed.

'Sounds like a mystery to me,' Rayra replied.

Breezy looked troubled as she wrapped herself in her insulated scarf — which was more like a tent in order to accommodate her length.

Roadrunner scanned the flea-inhabited forest; he saw a tigress inviting the chief of the fleas and his friends to ride on her back. Then he saw the fancy-looking beanpole — with the watery sapphire eyes that could melt any iron-clad heart — hopping around as if she too were a flea. Exhilarated, Roadrunner flew closer.

Meanwhile, a herd of cloned sheep grazed in the vicinity, their greasy wool yodelling-out for a flea to make a nest in. Disgusting and dim are the two D's that I am going to use to describe this army of shabby sheep; they were dim, disgusting and disturbing to any knowledgeable eye. They lurched forward, approaching the goofy-looking beanpole, spying a scarf of synthetic material neatly folded on the grass. The defenceless scarf was soon gobbled up by the plump, cloned animals, leaving the material that had strengthened Breezy in difficult situations in shreds. Roadrunner, who was not only a coward but ninety-nine-per-cent insensitive, felt no anger towards the sheep, nor any inclination to get involved. The Albatross of Mystery sensed trouble and felt fear, and this resulted in his rapid departure.

After guzzling most of Breezy's scarf, the would-be-chief-sheep Cud Greasole had an evil glint in her eye.

'Baaaaaaaaa aaaaaaa,' she bleated, making the earth tremble and laughing at the dancing fleas. She started eyeing them hungrily, studying them from their heads to their little flea feet. Cud fluttered her eyelashes in what she thought was a seductive manner and strutted over to the flea clan, flicking greasy locks of wool out of her humungous black eyes.

Now aware of the disappearance of her treasured scarf, Breezy scoured the forest for her prized possession. Turning back to face her flea friends and the greasy sheep clones, Breezy noticed that on each clone's head there was a familiar-looking pink ball of fluff: the remains of her ex-insulated scarf. Heartbroken, Breezy was rooted to the spot; she was so distraught that she couldn't bring herself to command her scraggly legs to race after those dim-witted dummies. Full of woe and in a state of shock, Breezy digested the bitter taste of injustice, bitter as Cud, who'd cruelly damaged her insulated scarf.

Breezy noticed the fleas being herded away by the sheep into the sunset and was confused. Couldn't they see past their cute button-noses and realise how manipulative the clones really were?

She was roused from her thoughts by a winged shadow passing over her, following the flea clan and clone herd. She sighed and suppressed a salty tear. Thinking on the bright and breezy side as always, she anticipated the arrival of Rayra. Circumstances had changed; it was Rayra's turn to help Breezy.

The next morning Rayra arrived home

with Scoffin, they'd had a wonderful time together, basking in the sunshine and gathering fresh carrots and sunflower seeds. On the way, they'd made a new acquaintance called Frax, who was an agreeable flea. He lived off fertiliser and had wished to join the clan of flirtatious fleas for a while, as he'd been searching for his soulmate.

The stillness of the forest made Rayra nervous. It was unlike the clan to wander off this early in the morning. She asked Frax to take care of sleeping Breezy whilst she and Scoffin searched for the clan. Rayra was confident that this was the right course of action, as she knew that it would be insensitive to wake Breezy as she needed rest. If Breezy's limbs didn't get enough rest they would ache — being long-limbed makes you fragile. Frax patiently kept watch, his little flea legs hanging over a low branch, eating gooseberries and studying Breezy's peaceful face.

The earth shuddered as a low 'baaaaaaaaa' swept across the landscape.

On hearing the noise, Scoffin and Rayra drew closer together. Rayra went first, closely followed by Scoffin covering her back. They stalked through the long grass, oblivious to what lay ahead. Rayra halted as she felt something brush her leg. She turned around... Scoffin had gone! She relaxed when she saw him reappear next to his friend Doono. Doono was the main betrayer of the clan and was now totally brainwashed by the grease-balls of wool, obeying everything Cud said. He had been so easily led by the herd because they gave off flirting pheromones, encouraging him to flirt back — after all, he *was* a flirtatious flea! To Doono, this was a game, a competition of the biggest flirts and show-offs, and, being one of the immature fleas in the clan, he didn't realise the danger he was in. At his age, Doono was interested in different species — especially if they were female — while Scoffin, who was more mature, saw straight through the woolly troublemakers. He was determined to drag Doono away, along with the rest of the clan. However, Scoffin's attempts to persuade Doono to leave the sheep were unsuccessful.

Rayra was fuming. She knew Doono had been manipulated by those miscreants and noticed shreds of Breezy's scarf on their greasy heads. Why had those unfashionable clones aggressively torn it apart? She knew that the herd were full of greasy intentions and they revelled in destruction. Rayra prepared to pounce on the sheep; she knew that Cud Greasole was behind this malicious act and she thought about wrenching the wool off Cud's unworthy skin — forgetting that she was now a vegetarian.

'You dirty little pile of knitting!' Rayra growled at the sneering Cud. 'How *dare* you take my friend's quality insulated scarf, something so beautiful and original, and transfer it to *your* own bland and blank head!' she snarled, her voice rising to an infuriated shriek.

'Excuse me? What *are* you anyway? An ickle whining kitten?' Cud replied mockingly. 'By the way, that look and those stripes are *so* last year! Get the picture?'

'Neither are dunderheads!' Scoffin interjected.

Cud ignored him. 'You, kitty-cat, are so low to the ground, just like your status in life,' she spat.

'You're the one stooping low, feeling resentment and jealousy of another's style and being an odious character for no reason!' Rayra paused to sharpen her claws, ready for the kill.

Meanwhile, Breezy had woken from her dreamless slumber and was firing questions at Frax about Rayra's whereabouts, when she spied the same bird again: the Albatross of Mystery. Breezy knew that seeing an albatross circling the air wasn't a good omen. She sprang to her feet, letting Frax jump on her shoulder. She ran like the wind, so fast that she could've easily outrun Roadrunner!

Seeing her friend about to pounce on Cud, Breezy cried, 'No Rayra! She's not worth it - besides, you're a veggie!'

Rayra froze, obeying her good friend.

Breezy took a deep breath and bellowed, 'Fleas, ATTACK!'

Tired of pleasing the notorious Cud and her greedy flock, the fleas caught the sheep by surprise, pouncing onto their matted backs, biting them hard. The petrified clones retreated, leaving their wool behind.

Doono was the only flea not partaking in the swarm; he'd decided to stick with Cud. Cud was more aggressive than before, as she hated the sight of that lanky Beanpole and her little tigress. Breezy, who was a peaceable creature, acted as a barrier between Cud, Rayra and Scoffin — the latter was attempting to shield Rayra with difficultly.

Breezy succeeded in protecting her friends, but in turn she suffered as Cud bent her into the shape of a coat hanger. The brittle beanpole collapsed onto the grass, unable to move.

Just when all hope seemed lost, the fighting fleas returned from defeating the herd and were more than ready to eliminate Cud and, unfortunately, Doono. Rayra and Scoffin licked each other's wounds whilst the fleas squeezed the grease out of the woolly coats that the herd had left behind. The grease was used to fry fresh carrots to make delicious carrot chips to revive the group.

Sadly, Breezy was still unconscious from the attack. Frax tended to her, feeding her gooseberries, hoping they would loosen her rigid limbs. Eventually they did but, nevertheless, she remained lifeless.

Frax slumped onto the grass, fearing Breezy's fate, when a mysterious-looking albatross crash-landed, dropping a clump of wool. Using his beak, Roadrunner stretched it over Breezy. It was a brand-new insulated scarf! Frax remained still, wondering what the strange bird would do next.

Roadrunner was unaware of the flea's presence; his eyes were fixed on Breezy's face, hoping to catch one last glimpse of those sapphire eyes. Breezy's eyelids fluttered open and she smiled at him, but before she could utter a brief 'thank you', Roadrunner vanished, afraid of commitment. The befuddled Breezy soon realised that her real saviour was Frax the gooseberry-wielder, who returned her smile and vowed to protect her always.

The smell of fried carrots reached Breezy's nose and she had an idea: she began to knit speedily back and forth from scraps of leftover wool until she had made a miniature kilt for each flea.

After modelling their kilts and celebrating, the fleas re-christened themselves "The Flea Clan of Frivolity". That night, Frax drank a whole bottle of fertiliser and transformed into a tall, handsome beanpole, fit to travel with Breezy and her friends.

Rob Dob and Periwinkle

Rob Dob was a teenage pixie who had extremely pointy ears and soft, pale blue eyes. The other fairies and pixies liked him because he was calm and sometimes mischievous. You could tell when he'd been mischievous, because a healthy-looking vein would come up from underneath his bobble hat and his clothes would have mud, dew and grass stains on them.

All fairies and pixies went to Sharson Puck III School in the centre of Myrtlemulberry, and even though it was a big school, everyone knew each other. However, each fairy and pixie had their own specific group. It took one very special fairy a year to find a group where she belonged. This was because, initially, she didn't know many people and went in and out of most of the groups. Her name was Periwinkle because her eyes were a mixture of blue and purple. Her face was thin with a mysterious air to it. She stood out from the crowd by wearing dresses and skirts that were unusual styles and colours — yet no matter how unusual her clothes were, they always matched. When she wasn't with her trustworthy friends Tulip and Rose, she floated along quietly, watching everyone else. Periwinkle was a true observer. She got to know people by watching them and listening to their conversations; this wasn't eavesdropping, it was merely her taking an interest in those around her.

When Periwinkle met Rob Dob she instantly took a liking to him because he was always up to something interesting. She tried talking to him between lessons. She really wanted him to like her, even though normally she didn't care about what other people thought. She noticed that Rob Dob loved to have fun but he was also very conscientious at school, which added to his charm.

One day, a girl called Wheyjel approached Periwinkle. She was the May Queen every year because everyone was afraid that if they didn't vote for her she would pick on them. Everyone stared at the two very different fairies, waiting in anticipation.

'Oh my dewdrops! That skirt is so ugly! Where did you get it from, a hole in the ground?' As Wheyjel said this she had to stand on tiptoes because she was so short.

Periwinkle gazed at her for a second and then, blushing angrily at this insult, with butterflies rising in her throat, she took a deep breath and said, 'Why don't you pick on someone your own size, Shorty?'

Rob Dob looked up from underneath his bobble hat and grinned. Wheyjel stomped off.

Every year at Sharson Puck III School there was a huge party, a bit like a disco. Rose, Tulip and Periwinkle had been working on their dresses for weeks. Periwinkle surprised her friends when she showed them her dress.

'It's so pretty!' Rose cried excitedly.

Tulip pressed her slight fingertips together. 'Umm… Yes it suits you, but…'

'What's wrong with it?' Periwinkle said, her voice high-pitched.

'Well…it's very plain compared with your other outfits,' Tulip explained.

'But even though it is plain, it looks great. Don't worry, everyone will love it!' Rose said encouragingly.

'I hope so,' Periwinkle sighed.

The gardens were decorated with rainbow-coloured lights, Chinese lanterns and dewdrops which sparkled on the freshly mown grass. A soft breeze blew across the outside of the tent where the party was held. Little cakes were spread across the tables and pink toadstools on sticks were served with spoonfuls of honey. Rose, Tulip and Periwinkle arrived wearing their long, flowing dresses. When the guest register had been taken and everyone was present, the party began.

Fairies, pixies and humans were mingling and flirting, laughing and twittering. Periwinkle preferred to dance with her friends. She had her own style of dancing as well as her own style of dress; she twirled and stepped gracefully along with the music, totally absorbed. Her silky dress circled around her, while the flowers in her hair bopped along to the disco beat. She was a blur of lavender and silver.

Rob Dob didn't dance. Instead, he visited each group in the tent — like Periwinkle at the start of the year — and listened to the latest gossip. When Periwinkle caught his eye, he looked at her and grinned. Suddenly the mischievous vein disappeared, and with a serious expression he removed his bobble hat and handed it to Wheyjel, who stared at him wide-eyed and open-mouthed.

He approached Periwinkle. 'Hi, are you having a good time?'

Periwinkle was startled and tripped over her dress, losing one of her sparkly shoes in the process. The shoe was catapulted into the air and landed with extreme force onto the head of the approaching Wheyjel, who lost her balance and fell to the floor. A crowd of girls swarmed around Wheyjel as she struggled to her feet.

Rob Dob's head and pointy ears emerged from the crowd and commotion and he returned to Periwinkle, gingerly placing the lost shoe onto her foot. Goosebumps appeared on Periwinkle's pale skin; she smiled and fell into Rob's gentle gaze.

'Thank you! To answer the question you asked me before, yes I am enjoying myself, this party rocks! I love to dance. Why don't you dance?' Periwinkle gabbled, beaming happily at him.

'I'm not really very good at it,' he replied, blushing.

Periwinkle smiled, her eyes sparking. 'I'll help you!'

Before Rob Dob could reply or step towards the mysterious, glamorous fairy, he was whisked off by Wheyjel; she had recovered from her fall and was still clutching Rob's hat. Periwinkle turned away and resumed dancing.

Rob Dob tried all evening to approach Periwinkle but the other fairies wouldn't leave him alone. All he could do was glance at Periwinkle dancing while he found himself surrounded by a group of immature, giggling fairies. He noticed that Periwinkle's dancing had also attracted a crowd of childish and stupid pixies. Periwinkle felt Rob's gaze upon her and her skin prickled as she returned his gaze. She made a face at Wheyjel, whose back was turned, causing Rob to grin mischievously.

Rob Dob was excited about seeing Periwinkle again and was so deep in thought that he forgot to meet Wheyjel to walk up to school with her. Wheyjel was furious, but Rob Dob didn't care. Periwinkle and schoolwork were the only things on his mind. As soon as Periwinkle arrived through an open window he grabbed a seat next to her.

They laughed and joked and Periwinkle's mysterious side was revealed. She wasn't popular, but Rob Dob loved her for who she was. The pair enjoyed school more and Periwinkle no longer struggled to please the other students. The following year she was voted May Queen. Wheyjel never bothered Periwinkle again.

Emma Dilemma:
Professional Problem
Solver

A newcomer had arrived at Sharson Puck III School. Her name was Lily Lilt and she was an elf. Lily felt uncomfortable about being new, but decided to try her best to make this school her home and to forge lasting friendships. However, nervous Lily felt it would be best to explore the school before meeting people.

Most of the students at the magical high-school were friendly and helpful, but, as in all places, there were a few unhelpful individuals. Lily was having trouble finding the headmistress' office, which she'd been told to report to. Confused and in need of help, she asked a passing warlock if he knew where it was.

His rat-like features arranged themselves into a grin.

'Oh yes, it's through that door and up the stairs,' he said, stifling a chuckle with his sleeve before turning his back on her.

'Thanks!' Lily replied, thinking nothing of the weird character.

He was right: there were stairs. They were wooden and went round in a spiral. She carefully climbed whilst nerves tied knots in her stomach. Ahead of her was a massive room with a long glass window looking down on the front of the school. She thought it was a strange location for an office. The room was strangely empty apart from a cardboard box carelessly dumped in the middle, along with a wardrobe and chest of drawers. No desk. Lily was curious about the battered box and couldn't leave without peeking inside. She knew that this place wasn't the headmistress' office and she was right; the warlock that told her to go upstairs was a trickster and a bad representative of the school. It was a shame that he was the first student she met. Fortunately, Lily was hopeful and believed that everything happened for a reason: she was meant to end up here and look inside the box.

Luckily for Lily, the contents of the box were not deadly — unlike the legendary Pandora's Box, which released the evils of the world. As she drew closer to the box, she saw a piece of tape holding up a tea-stained sign which read: "*Residence of Miss Emma Dilemma, Professional Problem Solver*". Judging from the swift, scruffy lettering, she could tell that the box's inhabitant was a pixie. Pixies are hot-tempered and impatient, so Lily thought it strange that one should be in a job that required tolerance.

Trying to be polite and considerate, Lily knocked on the box. There was a groan from within and then a tanned, podgy pixie hand pushed the cardboard flaps up.

'Who're you?' Miss Emma Dilemma demanded.

'I'm new — my name is Lily.'

'Well, what's the problem, Lil?'

'I don't have one. I was confused and found myself in here.'

'That's very common with visitors.'

'Well, actually, I'm staying,' Lily said meekly.

'You won't last very long unless you know the ropes,' Emma replied bluntly.

'I've just arrived. I'm sure I'll get used to it and make some friends, this isn't a problem as I mentioned before.'

'You definitely need my help,' Emma exclaimed; she had a talent for identifying a person's worries within five minutes of meeting them.

'It looks like I've found a friend already,' Lily replied gratefully.

'And with my help you'll find many more,' Emma said, enthusiastic about helping a new client.

'That's great...but I'm not looking for instant friends who are...'

'Superficial? Oh there are a lot of girls like that here, and everywhere else! Let me see... You want friends that will last? Am I right?'

'Yes, that's exactly it! You really are a professional,' Lily said happily.

'I know, I know.' Emma inspected her shiny nails thoughtfully. 'Now, my idea is to test people...or maybe just fairies ...'

'I don't care what creatures they are!' Lily replied, shocked.

'At least you're not fussy; I've had worse clients. The plan is to find out how true they are. Am I right in thinking that you'd like friends who stand out from the crowd?' Emma queried.

'Yes. I had some bad experiences at my last school,' Lily added quietly.

'That's sorted then, leave it to me. Here's my card if you ever need me.'

'But what're you going to do?' Lily asked.

'You'll see. Go — I've other clients to see,' the pixie retorted impatiently.

'One last question. What is this place?'

'A closet. I live here, you know!' Emma replied with the same air of annoyance.

'Do you have lessons at the school like everyone else?' Lily questioned further.

'No. The school employed me to help other students *and* because I'm such a *nice* person. I won't charge you, Lil. Consider it a consultation. Now, GET OUT!' Emma had lost her temper; it was clear she was only interested in her job and had no time for small-talk.

Lily backed away, muttered 'thank you' and watched the short-tempered pixie disappear into the box.

Lily's first lesson of making "heavenly cakes" was cut short when Miss Emma Dilemma walked in. Heads turned — even their teacher froze — waiting for the chubby pixie to speak.

'This lesson has been cancelled. Follow me, *now*, to the Assembly Hall,' Miss Emma Dilemma said.

Lily's classmates whispered to each other, but no one dared question Emma. After a minute of walking, Emma Dilemma stopped abruptly. The line of students looked like life-sized dominoes as they crashed into each other.

'Why are you boys still following us?' Emma spat.

The boys were silent.

Emma muttered under her breath, puffed her cheeks out and bellowed, 'Come on, then! Don't keep me and the rest of the school waiting.' She scowled at a short fairy whose hair could only be described as too shiny and perfect. This fairy's name was Wheyjel; she was a popular and nasty student in Lily's year group.

Soon after Emma's shouting, they reached the Assembly Hall. It was a beautiful, circular room with homely tropical plants and cushioned chairs in it. The walls were pale yellow and the windows had bright blue curtains.

Lily sat down on one of the cushioned chairs. In the centre of the circular room were three ugly, long-nosed goblins. They looked down their long noses at the students and sneered as though they had been told a hilarious private joke. Emma Dilemma entered last and strode into the centre to join the visitors. She greeted them coolly and clasped each of their scaly hands in turn, before turning to face the female students, her platform shoes sparkling.

'Girls, these people are fashion experts. They work for Daily Dew and Unicorn Fashion magazines.'

A few of the girls gasped. Lily had never read those silly magazines, but these goblins didn't look like fashion experts to her. She knew that Emma Dilemma had something up her sleeve — or, rather, hidden beneath her platform shoes.

'Now, I know that some of you girls are very fashion conscious, so I persuaded the teachers to let you have an assembly with these experts.'

Lily heard a few groans behind her and whispers of, 'They took us out of heavenly cakes for *this*?!'

The ugliest of the three goblins stepped

forward. 'Hello, I am Lawrence. Thank you for the marvellous intro! Now my colleagues have a fantabulously *fashionable* tip for your school.'

'Let's hear it!' a group of fairies, who looked like clones of each other, chorused.

Another of the long-nosed creatures stepped forward and addressed them, speaking in a common street twang. 'Oh, hiya babes. Yeah, well, we've been thinkin' that ya'll should all give skirt wearing a rest, ya know what I'm a sayin'?'

The third goblin pushed the second out the way and cleared his throat. 'Yes, you see legs are more *modern* covered up — also, trousers and stripy socks are soooo in. The main cut of trouser this summer is woollen tartan flares, which are best accompanied with long stripy woollen socks and snow boots.'

'Thank you, sir. If you want to remain fashionable and cool, I suggest that you follow their inexpert advice.'

Most people had switched off by then and did not hear Emma lower her voice on the word 'inexpert'. She winked at Lily, before exiting the room along with the long-nosed goblins.

Dazed and confused, the girls hurried to their second lesson which was actually their relaxation period. Lily didn't quite see how this "fashion tip" would make her find true friends, but then again Emma Dilemma's strange ideas *had* earned her the title of a professional. She would just have to trust her.

The goblins' tip had obviously been taken onboard as lots of female fairies, pixies, ogres, trolls, goblins, dwarves, elves and others were now wearing ridiculous woollen tartan flares and snow boots. As the sun's rays baked the grass dry, students wearing the outfit recommended by the goblins, stamped their feet in order to create a breeze and, in doing so, stepped on one another's wide flares, sending each other hurtling towards the ground before scratching their over-heated legs. Those in desperate need of ventilation cut holes into their trousers. Others decided to strut and bear the heat, ignoring those around them who grew faint. Lily watched them and thought how silly all of this was.

'The things people do for fashion!' Emma chuckled from behind Lily. Lily jumped in surprise.

'I thought you were busy and had clients to see,' Lily replied good-humouredly.

'Yes, I'm with an important one right now. Look, keep watching these girls and see which ones don't keep up with the so-called "fashion". They are your real friends, or at least some of them are.'

'How did you figure that out?' Lily asked.

'Well, I am amazing, you've got to admit. It is common sense. Real people are not sheep; they wear what they want to, when they want to, even if it isn't "in season". They don't care about being popular. I see you're still in your skirt — that's good.'

'So you wear those platforms because you want to?' Lily was curious.

'Well…it is *good* to keep up with the fairy fashions… They are always flattering, even for a professional problem-solving pixie,' Emma said nervously.

'I see…' Lily replied, about to start a debate.

Emma cut her off hurriedly, 'Good. Then my work here is done.'

A week after the assembly, Wheyjel looked ridiculous and so did her group of clones. Lily found this funny, as did Emma Dilemma — especially as it was summer.

A group of mixed elves and fairies saw Lily laughing and approached her. One was wearing a bright pink skirt and a fuchsia top, another a turquoise flowing dress and the other, a short, pleated flowery skirt.

'Hi,' the elf said, smiling warmly at Lily.

Then the fairy with fiery sapphire eyes said, 'This rule is so fake and...absurd!' She looked extremely serious.

Then the one wearing the turquoise dress introduced them all, saying, 'That's Rizz, I'm Amber and this is Dawn.'

'I'm Lily.'

The pink-clad fairy called Rizz stared moodily at the poppies in the school garden, which made the group laugh. It seemed that Lily had found her new friends. Emma Dilemma had helped with her stupid rule but Lily was wise and would have found her friends anyway. She was glad to have met Emma, who was both funny and scary at the same time.

Lily Lilt is still at the school, along with all the other characters mentioned, and is a changed elf; one who feels very at home at Sharson Puck III School.

Twelve eyes are better than

none

Thrice a week, seven youths would meet out of duty. As time progressed, they overcame all manners of shyness and became a fellowship, battling against the monotony of their English teacher.

Bright Eyes, a student pursuing a career in photography, was very photogenic; he had piercing dark blue eyes that penetrated through light coloured hair, which failed to mask his striking stare.

Camel Eyes was a friend of Bright Eyes. He was a long-lashed, flirtatious gnome, not unlike the fleas that Rayra and Breezy had met on their adventures. He was an entertainer, outrageous and at home in all social circles and situations.

Wonder Eyes was not a friend of the above but an acquaintance. He was part mole and part dormouse, colour-blind yet witty, although he was asleep ninety percent of the time.

Frog Eyes was a female gnome with dark and deadly straight hair; she was called so because of her large, questioning, mossy eyes. She was always actively involved in conversation.

Shimmer Eyes was an alluring merrow; she had long, metallic blue talons and shimmering dust over her eyelids. Shimmer was tall and sylph-like, always glamorous with a gleaming plumage of hair. Her character was vibrant, yet volatile. She was quick to turn sour but easily sweetened up by Camel Eyes — who was usually the person who had irritated her in the first place.

Aware Pupils was a slightly more complex character to decipher. She was a tawny coloured cat who was more anxious than the others to listen to their monotonous teacher, but would regularly tune in to the discussions of her companions and surprise them by joining in when they had forgotten she was there.

All of the above had nicknames referring to eyes, except for Gnat. Gnat was a gnat with small, piggish features and a chortling laugh; when she spoke she made a nasal sound, and when she did not speak her mouth hung open and the sound of saliva breaking down chewing gum could be heard. Common noises made by Gnat, other than those already mentioned, were 'Wot?', and the occasional dislikeable snort at someone else's expense.

As you will already know, a gnat is like a midge or a mosquito. It feeds off another, biting and sucking its blood, leaving a repulsive lump of a bite that itches and irritates the skin. This is how Gnat made people feel.

The last character that deserves a full introduction here is Harold — or "Sir" to the gang. He was a Pterodactyl, all brown and wrinkly except for his hairy, speckled head. He was the oldest teacher at Sharson with a beer belly and a Cheshire Cat grin. Many thought his career as an English teacher was wasted, as he would have made a fine Shakespearian Actor. Instead, he taught them the meaning of the books they studied in detail and rambled on about totally unrelated subjects. For example, he compared the balcony scene in *Romeo and Juliet* to car accidents because he was convinced that Romeo was as reckless as today's drivers.

When this occurred, Camel Eyes would turn to Aware Pupils, scrunch his nose up and ask, 'What's he on about now?' and she would retrace the monologue all the way back to the origin of *Romeo and Juliet*.

Today was no ordinary lesson; it was Speaker's Day. Once a term, the English department of Sharson Puck III School would invite people from all over Sharson to come in and give a talk to the class about themselves. The stranger and scarier the speakers were, the better. Speakers in the past had included a man with fangs like Dracula, who smelt strongly of aftershave and was a businessman, and a tubby primary school teacher with a glued-on-smile and hair like a clown, who had a pneumonic for everything — and those were just the sane cases.

If the speaker was female, Camel Eyes would charm her and Frog Eyes would try to impress her. If the speaker was male, Shimmer Eyes would sparkle at him and

Bright Eyes would observe him closely. Aware Pupils and Wonder Eyes were always the same: Wonder would get some sleep or pull out a sandwich to munch on and Aware would listen and formulate an opinion, which all Eyes would discuss at any available chance. Gnat, however, would be actively involved in the speaker's speech, asking dim-witted and unrelated questions, such as 'where do you live?' or 'what's your favourite colour?', or make tactless comments such as 'you don't look like a model' or 'all chefs must be fat.' In these cases, worried glances would be exchanged and Harold would step in and contradict Gnat or make a joke out of the whole thing.

It was a regular day: double maths spent working out areas and simultaneous equations, laughing and peeking in the back of the textbook for answers. Then it was time for English — a relief, as always, for Aware Pupils. Greeted with a hug from Bright Eyes and a flash of a camera, the lesson was about to begin. Shimmer Eyes applied dazzle dust onto her glossy lids. Meanwhile, Frog Eyes frowned at her own reflection whilst shielding herself from the iridescent light rays coming from Shimmer's hair.

At that moment, wearing Elton John style sunglasses, Camel Eyes made his entrance. Brushing hair off his face, he jumped on Shimmer. She began to snarl but then, upon seeing his curling lashes, grinned and kissed him lightly on the cheek. As the girls were recovering and Aware Pupils was getting comfy in her seat, Wonder Eyes slammed his stuff onto the table, nodded his head in greeting and began to gnaw at a French baguette. Bright Eyes photographed this, of course, while Aware Pupils wondered if Sir would ever notice Wonder Eyes eating in his lessons. Maybe Harold did notice but was unsure of who the culprit was, as it was difficult to make out the dormouse from behind the loaded baguette.

'Is Miss Piggy here today?' Shimmer Eyes pushed Camel off her lap and beamed (literally) at Aware.

'No she's off ill — she's got a terrible sty on her eye!' Aware mewed theatrically. Bright Eyes grinned.

'What? How can she have a whole pigsty on her eye?' Wonder emerged from his sandwich.

'It's a pun,' Frog Eyes yawned.

Gnat entered, chortling and wiggling

her bum around. The girls stared in disgust. Wonder Eyes stared hard at his sandwich and offered Aware Pupils a sardine. Camel Eyes watched with interest, while Bright Eyes hid behind his hair.

'Hiya guys! Scnorf,' Gnat let out nasally. 'Ew! Are you eatin' sardines?! That is sooo dis…erm —'

'— gusting?' Wonder Eyes offered

'Revolting?' Aware had her Thesaurus out.

'Yeah, what she said. You're, like, in my maths group, right?' she said, singling out Aware.

'Yes, and dance,' Aware replied coldly.

'No, I don't think so…' Gnat had her nose in the air.

'I am. I'm the one who can't dance, remember?'

'Oh yeah! You haven't been in Mardi Gras or anything, that's why. Unlike me. Anyways, I was wondering if you could, like, help me with my maths homework and maybe dance theory — it's well solid!' (Meaning "very difficult" to us normal folk).

'Well, as you said, she is utterly useless at dance so why would you need her help?' Wonder Eyes spat.

'You are so right! Hey, Snot Eyes! You're in the top set for maths, what about you? Do my homework!'

'Do it yourself!' Frog Eyes yelled.

'I'll do it for you,' Camel fluttered his lashes.

'Really?' Gnat was hopeful

'If you become my girlfriend.'

'LOSER!' she spat.

'Just kidding, you'd spoil my image. Bright Eyes'll do it for you,' Camel Eyes said.

'Yeah, if you get off our table and leave us alone...' Bright Eyes replied underneath his hair.

'And take back what you said about Aware, she can pirouette ten times around you when it comes to English!' Shimmer's eyes flashed — and not just because of her makeup.

Gnat shut up, afraid of having to move seats to a place where she did not feel superior.

Aware smiled her thanks as paper balls zoomed across the room. One hit Gnat and knocked the chewing gum out of her mouth and into Wonder's sandwich. He did not notice. There was a click and everyone froze. The door slammed against the wall as

Harold swept into the classroom. Paper balls were picked up and chewing gum spat out. Shortly afterwards, there was a knock on the door; the speaker had arrived.

Sir's brow wrinkled when they entered. A man and a woman, who were both very hairy.

'Maybe they are starring in "Lost", as new characters in the last series!' Gnat squealed.

Shimmer Eyes grinned at the visitors. The woman smiled at Bright Eyes as he moved his hair out of his face to look, before letting his fringe fall again. Wonder was asleep, while Camel Eyes and Frog Eyes were singing and playing air guitar; both they and Wonder received a kick from Aware.

'Wake UP! There are two of them today.'

The male visitor spoke to Sir timidly, 'I'm sorry, but my wife decided to come and I couldn't stop her.'

'I understand,' Harold replied, with his Cheshire Cat grin. 'Ok, my Chicken Kormas! (Harold often referred to his students as items of food right before break) This is our — sorry, *these* are today's speakers. Without further ado, let the talks begin! I trust you will all listen carefully and ask questions at the end.'

'Oh. Hello. My name is Argerr Bussilton. I am a University Lecturer and in my spare time a gourmet cook.'

'Ooh!' some of the girls said. The man, with his butterscotch tie, sandals and grey fleece, blinked and continued.

The gang were prepared now that Argerr had made his introduction; Frog Eyes passed around cookies her little brother had made, Camel took six and Bright Eyes scrutinised them before deciding on grapes instead. Aware, who was watching the speaker like a hawk, felt something cold on her ear, a grape had been thrown at her.

'Hey, Frogs! I wasn't ready!'

'Here,' Bright Eyes passed one to her.

'Thanks.'

It was time to ask questions.

'What do you lecture on?' This came from one of the intelligent minds in the class.

'My speciality is American Presidents and their diet. To be a good leader you need a good diet, it's scientifically proven.' He stared at them all eating grapes, thoughtfully. Sir took no notice, as he was taking notes.

'What did you eat for breakfast?' Gnat bellowed. Shimmer rolled her eyes, creating little lights on the ceiling like a disco ball.

'A banana.'

'Lunch?' Camel asked.

'Banana baguette.'

'Dinner?' Bright Eyes raised his eyebrows, wondering whether it was a new diet like Special K.

'Barbequed bananas, of course.' His eyes lit up more than they had done when he explained his lecture topic. Then the smile was replaced by a groan.

Bright Eyes and Camel Eyes exchanged glances. Aware looked concerned, along with Shimmer and Frog, and Wonder stopped chewing.

Gnat, who had no gum to mash up, did the only other thing she could do, and said, 'I think he's got a hairball! Look out for banana spew!'

Sir flew over to Argerr but his wife stepped in.

'Mi, mi! My darling's gote a migraine. Vud you like to seet down 'oney?' she spoke as if talking to a china baby. She wore brown blusher and red lipstick, had cropped hair, a large nose and a yellow bandana.

'What a voice!' Camel Eyes whispered to Bright Eyes, his eyes fixed on the woman's red lips.

'Yeah, she sure makes everything sound appealing and gooey, like chocolate,' Bright Eyes said, nodding in agreement.

'Except she's less appealing than chocolate,' Wonder joined in.

This was "Guy Talk". The girls looked at their nails thoughtfully and watched the tall stick of a woman make her way to Harold's desk.

'Personally, I reckon she's a man-eater,' Aware commented.

'Yeah, she's got claws, man,' Frog Eyes agreed.

Bright Eyes had now emerged from his hair. 'I have to admit, she scares me.'

'I bet she's into bananas too, have you seen how thin she is?' Shimmer criticised.

'Nah, she's mysterious…' Camel Eyes said dreamily.

'Got any more of them grapes?' Wonder Eyes cut in.

'Maybe I should just run on bananas — then I could wear my new bikini,' Shimmer pondered.

'I'd like to see that!' Camel turned his attention away from the woman for a moment.

'What if you start to look like a banana?' Aware enquired thoughtfully.

'Yeah man, that's not a good shape!' Frog Eyes said.

'And you'd be more susceptible to bruises,' Bright Eyes continued.

'And people would want to eat you to get slim,' Wonder chomped.

'I would advise you, Shimmer, to hang out in a bunch, that way you'd be safer from an attack by University Lecturers...' Camel Eyes grinned.

'And they are not ripe company!' Aware concluded. Everyone giggled.

'Wot?' Gnat pouted.

'So, Mrs Bussilton, would you like to tell my adolescents about your occupation?' Sir gestured around the room and offered her a chair next to her husband.

'Dat would be lovely!'

'Whoa!' Camel Eyes sighed in awe. Her lipstick curved inwards into a smile, revealing immaculate fang-like teeth.

'Ugh!' Bright Eyes responded.

'I am a tour guide in Las Paaalmas in Grand Canaaaria. I have been dere for ten years, I learnt English and have been taking tours ever seeence.'

'Wow that's amaaazing! What it is like in Las Palmas?' Camel Eyes boomed, fluttering his eyelashes at her.

She blew him a kiss. After that, her husband seemed to watch the red-lipped stick insect like a monkey watches his bananas.

This was a bad question to ask!

'*Vot a shaaarming young man! In Las Paaalmas we have hotels end potatoes vhich come viv a moho sauce. But da main attraction to da beauty of Las Paaalmas is the bananas.*'

Camel Eyes nodded along, looking scintillated. This was a very, very bad idea.

'*Oh da bananas! Ve have many banana plantations and ve grow dvarf bananas and vhite and seelver bananas...*'

'I think they understand, Jangez,' Harold interrupted wearily.

'*Vel dey can all take a leaflet on the Banana Tours.*' She flashed her fangs, pulled out a banana from her pocket, threw it at her husband and left with him trailing behind her. Harold collapsed into the now vacant chair.

'Sir...' Gnat moaned, urgently.

'Yes?' Harold sighed, stretching out his

wings.

'You forgot to ask us if we had any questions!' she hissed, somehow snorting at the same time.

Harold smiled over-sweetly. 'I'll tell you what, Gnat, go and catch up with them if you want and I'm sure they'll answer all of your burning questions.' His voice was now louder, his tone dry. 'And you can spit that gum out too, while you're there. When you're done, we'll be waiting for you.'

Gnat realised that if she left she would be out of a lesson and maybe she could trade her gum in for some that was banana-flavoured. Sir wanted her to go. After all, he said they'd wait for her. So she went.

Previously angry but now amused and shocked at Gnat's obedience, Harold roared with laughter along with the majority of the other students. He then decided to go and get her but got side-tracked and began to discuss the similarities between *A Midsummer Night's Dream* and *Spider-Man*.

Two hours later – having visiting the university where Argerr worked - Gnat returned to find that Harold's was classroom empty. She soon forgot why she was there and left to buy some bubblegum.

From that day forth, Speakers Day was banned. Harold preferred to have his class giving talks to each other, which was a scary event for the first table picked, but the rest were let off as he soon forgot about the speeches and would move onto another topic. The Eyes weren't sad that their days of observing 'Speakers' were over, as they had a whole portfolio full of all the ones that they had met previously, and this kept them entertained when there was nothing weird and wonderful to discuss.

Village ties

A duo of snowy geese called Chatter and Banter contemplated the weather. A hail storm was approaching the village of Arbsitchy and Mr J. Long. Flagpole held up a red tulip, a signal of bad weather.

Chatter and Banter fluffed their feathers moodily as they sheltered in the reeds. They'd have to wait until tomorrow for their perm and the week's gossip. Both were furious with Weather for interrupting their prying schedule! *Weather was such a disorganised woman, totally fickle and flamboyant! She had access to the latest gossip but no desire to listen. At least we appreciate the finer things in life*, they thought.

The village know-it-alls were so preoccupied with The Amazing Tulip's wedding plans that they hadn't thought to research the identity of their new neighbours.

Chatter and Banter were mistaken about Weather. She may have caused them to cancel their weekly appointment, but she had done them a favour. As the geese sipped cordial and knitted some jumpers, three gangly trolls grunted along, resistant to sharp pieces of rock bouncing off their boulder-like shoulders.

***

Homan, a compulsive ice-cream devourer and ex-advisor to King Uglous, found love after leaving Sharson Castle. She'd been squelching through the swamps, feeling cold, depressed and hungry — it was two in the morning and she had a craving for Smarties — when she saw him. Her love was a very unlikely troll named Jojobo Sparoo who, at the time, was snoozing on a lilo. Homan joined him and found they shared similar interests; sleeping, eating and a fear of anything that moved. Homan loved trudging through life with Jojobo and couldn't wait for them to move to Arbsitchy.

The only problem was their son, Edmund…
How would he evaluate the situation?

Edmund the Evaluator was also a troll, and like most trolls he was tall and muscular, but unlike most trolls, he read philosophy and wore stripy ties and shiny shoes. He had few possessions, making moving easy—he'd already moved swamp-hut four times. Most teenagers would find this hard, but not Edmund. Edmund grew accustomed to people with time and only had trouble moving away from places that he'd lived in for years. Edmund's intellect had certainly not originated from his parents; the only quality he inherited from his father was awkwardness around people. He was painfully shy and had difficulty making small-talk. However, he was an expert at single word answers and grunts like his father. Edmund's mother also had a gift which Edmund had inherited: she could sense with her fingertips when food was nearby and the type of food it was. Her son didn't need to touch objects, he just knew what they felt like. One of Edmund's possessions was a keyboard that he carried in his mind; he could imagine the keys and make silent music.

Homan and Jojobo tramped on, watching their son with anxiety — he was wearing his waterproof tie and drinking from his flask of tea — as they neared their new home.

***

Chatter and Banter had dozed off. Normally at this hour they'd take turns to look through the reeds in the garden, watching villagers come and go while theorising about the whereabouts of those who dared venture out of the village. They hadn't left the village for ten years. It was their duty to survey all goings-on in their territory. So, perhaps it wasn't such a bad thing that the elderly geese missed a most irregular sight: a trio of grubby trolls stomping past, clutching soggy bin bags. They would've thought that their rubbish had come back to haunt them for forgetting to put the bin out for collection on Friday.

***

Breezy the Beanpole left her home, but with every intention of returning to the flea forest where she and Rayra lived. Breezy was

Chatter and Banter's only visitor. She had incredible stamina and could sit for hours with the geese, discussing the usefulness of her insulated scarf. Her hollow legs enabled her to drink a colossal volume of tea, which was their sole advantage. Rather than sit, Breezy had to perch in a position as ladylike as her lengthy form would permit. Each time Breezy visited she tried a different blend of tea and a new scarf awaited her. The reason for Chatter and Banter's generosity towards Breezy was that she brought tales from foreign lands, was born in Arbsitchy and was a friend of the respectable Amazing Tulip.

That evening, Edmund attended a clairvoyant meeting where the locals studied tea leaves for meaning. Meanwhile, Breezy took Chatter and Banter dancing after tea. Without a partner, she swirled across the events room and twirled her scarf, accidentally hitting a few couples as she moved. Breathless, she sat down and flicked through her pocket dictionary. She had a passion for words and trusted their meanings. The first word she saw was "eccentricity". This made her smile, as the village was indeed an eccentric place, to hold a clairvoyant meeting adjacent to a dance class! The dictionary was her guide to the future. The words revealed how her visit would be: surprising, civilised and bizarre. The first two words fit, but the last? Breezy reopened the musty book and found the next set of words even more ambiguous: passive and rewarding. These words didn't seem to coincide, but the dictionary hadn't failed her before.

After the class, Breezy peeked into the clairvoyant room. Charts on the wall marked the position of the planets and there were books with titles like *What's it all about?* Breezy smiled; to her, this was a waste of time, searching for scientific or spiritual theories to explain everything. She didn't linger to ponder what she was missing.

*****

Weather was feeling better; the sky was a contented blue with no foreboding clouds to hide the stars. The geese gabbled about the church organ, which had had a hymn sheet lodged in the pipes and had made a most peculiar sound throughout 'All things bright and beautiful.' Breezy's legs began to droop; the tea was comforting and she felt tired but she couldn't sleep, it was bad etiquette. Besides, she'd hardly spoken in the past three hours and she had her own tales to tell.

'Chatter, you said that next door was for sale again?'

'Yes,' began Chatter, 'but —'

'People never seem to stay long *there*,' Banter finished.

'Quite right! Have you seen the wind turbines? No one can put up with a view like that for long!' Chatter said knowingly.

'I'm sure,' Breezy commented, used to this sort of talk. 'Is anyone living there now?' She seized the chance to ask questions, whilst she still had it.

Usually, Chatter and Banter would grin smugly and dish out details about their new neighbours. They'd had many, which all soon became ex-neighbours — and not purely because of the wind turbines. However, this time the geese sat and glared at one another. No one spoke. Chatter and Banter were ashamed that they'd overlooked an opportunity for fresh gossip. The geese's reputation was somewhat salvaged by a timely knock on the door. Both began to knit furiously in synchronisation, ignoring the visitor. Breezy untangled her legs from underneath the tea-table and went to the door.

Wrapping her latest scarf around her protectively, Breezy opened the oak door. On the other side stood a gangling adolescent male, looking rather worried and perplexed by Breezy's fluffy pink legwarmers which, had they been worn by a normal-sized female, would've been waist-high.

'Hello!' Breezy said brightly, the fresh air making her feel more awake.

'Hello,' was the bland response. The youth straightened his red and brown tie.

'Can I help you?' Breezy enquired.

'Do you have any coffee?' the visitor asked matter-of-factly.

'Why don't you come in? I'm a guest here so I'll have to ask.'

There was a pause from the tie-adjustor before a brief response. 'Right.'

The youth entered and surveyed the scene; two geese poised serenely with what seemed to be a pair of silver needles, scrutinising him over the top of their glasses. Edmund thought he was seeing double, until he noticed the different coloured rims of their glasses.

'Banter?' Breezy began.

'Yes, dear?'

'Do you have any coffee?'

'I think there's some in the pantry, it's —'

'Next to the packet of crumpets,' Chatter chipped in.

'I won't be a minute!' Breezy motioned for the guest to sit down.

Their visitor gulped. He knew a conversation was on the way.

'I'm Chatter,' Chatter said as she shook his hand formally.

'Edmund,' he replied dryly.

Banter then shook his hand, introducing herself. 'Banter.'

'You're a *coffee drinker*, are you, Edmund?' Chatter said coldly.

Edmund stared, processed the question and responded, 'No.'

'Oh. Banter drinks *coffee*, I suppose I'll allow her one fault!' Chatter replied jokingly.

'Right.' Edmund showed no signs of communicating further.

'What's the coffee for?' Banter enquired reproachfully.

'My dad drinks it.'

'So I'm not the only one around here!' Banter clucked. 'Are you from here? I can't say I've seen you before.'

'We just moved in.'

Chatter and Banter exchanged a glance, shocked. Their neighbour seemed an intelligent fellow, although not much fun as far as conversation went. Maybe he was shy? They would introduce him to some of their friends, surely no one could be that disconnected from the flow of discussion on a daily basis!

Breezy entered carrying a jar of coffee, blissfully unaware that she was holding it upside down.

'Let me help you, dear,' Banter exclaimed. Edmund could already sense coffee granules on the pale carpet.

'I'm fine, really!' Breezy passed the jar to Edmund, who fumbled and failed to hold the jar for more than a second before it toppled out of his large hands onto the carpet. For once, it wasn't Breezy who performed this clumsy act, but Edmund.

Chatter arched her brows and frowned.

'I'm so sorry! It's completely my fault,' Breezy gushed, blushing, before the geese had a chance to squawk their annoyance. 'I was holding the jar upside down and the lid hinge is weak.'

'It wasn't your fault. My hands have

a tendency to drop things before I can properly grasp them.' The words had filtered out through Edmund's tight lips. He'd uttered more than one sentence!

'I'm Breezy,' she smiled.

'Edmund. I live next door. Thanks for the coffee.'

Yet again, more than one sentence!

***

That night, the three companions discussed the new arrivals.

'A nice lad,' Banter commented.

'Troll,' Chatter corrected. 'Totally misguided.'

'Why?' Banter asked.

'Lack of social skills.'

'I thought he did rather well, the poor creature was shy!' Banter said.

Breezy chuckled at the way they talked about villagers, as though they were exhibits in a museum.

'I did like his tie, I must say!' Banter said.

'In my opinion, a scarf would be much better for this time of year. Wouldn't you say so, Breezy?'

Breezy nodded.

'I bet his mother and father are interesting people,' Banter began, changing the topic.

'Interesting?!' Chatter squawked. 'People who send their offspring out in the dark to stock up on supplies? People who bring their offspring up to be monosyllabic?'

'That's not a bad thing, dear. It shows he's disciplined,' Banter argued.

'We'll invite the whole family to tea and see for ourselves,' Chatter concluded.

'Isn't it a bit early for that? They just moved in,' Breezy said.

'They're our neighbours, for Weather's sake!' Chatter said tetchily.

'Right,' Breezy and Banter chorused with humour.

***

Imagine Homan's surprise when an invitation edged with gold reed found its way through their letterbox.

'Jojobo, love, we've been invited next door for tea!'

She was excited; it was years since she'd received a formal invitation. Her husband merely grunted in response.

'No eating beforehand! I'll arrive on time

with an empty stomach!' she said, bursting with joy.

Jojobo made a series of groans, which meant he wasn't coming — he had a lecture in trollish on mushrooms that day. Homan wondered whether Edmund would accompany her. She constantly worried about her son. After all, he was their first child and she wanted to get things right.

Edmund was uncertain. This occurred a lot. He couldn't comprehend the situation. Gold reed on an invite? What was the point? It'd end up in the bin! Despite his confusion, he loved his mother dearly and wanted to support her. Sometimes she was a little too much, whereas he was a little too little. Edmund evaluated, speculated and made a decision. He would go, but not because he wanted to see the smiley beanpole, but because he had forgotten what afternoon tea felt like. Content with this, he played a chromatic scale, feeling the notes in his head.

***

Bleary-eyed Breezy walked into a shocking sight: the geese with a telescope, taking turns to unashamedly peer at the villagers. Today, their main focus was the Amazing Tulip's wedding dress and rehearsal lunch. Neither goose was shamefaced when Breezy raised her eyebrows, but instead invited her to join them;

'There's another telescope in the desk drawer, dear!'

Breezy couldn't understand their obsession with the wedding. After all, they were invited, so why see the dress now? Especially when there might be more intriguing events taking place, on the other side of the wall.

'If I were you, I'd keep watch on the newcomers, you know, just to check on them,' Breezy whispered suggestively.

Banter waddled upstairs to spy on the neighbours, while Chatter kept her eye out for the wedding dress. Breezy went to the post office to send Rayra news of her holiday in Arbsitchy.

Breezy knew that Rayra loved a good gossip like Chatter and Banter, but she wasn't obsessed by it. Breezy included details of Edmund's visit and a description of his tie. Rayra reacted how Breezy predicted she would and now wanted to meet Edmund for herself. After their previous adventure with the greasy sheep, Rayra had discovered a passion for designing unique and beautiful clothes and wondered if she could do some 'work' on Edmund to re-evaluate and revitalise his style. Breezy wasn't sure how Chatter and Banter would react to Rayra visiting, no matter how lovely her manners were. She'd have to make it seem as though Rayra's presence at the tea party was their idea, not hers. Rayra's visit would be a blessing in disguise.

***

The invite contradicted itself, which troubled Edmund. There it was, lying on top of *The Truth about Fish* with posh lettering, which read: '*Guests are to come dressed in casual clothes.*' Contradiction was a most hideous thing.

As he cycled around the village, he wondered if they really had liked his tie, or if long johns would be more appropriate for the occasion. Edmund didn't dress casually; he wore the same smart clothing all the time, so to him casual was no different from smart.

Miraculously, Breezy convinced the geese to let Rayra stay the night and join them for tea. It hadn't been hard, but it hadn't been exactly easy either. Breezy had to tell a few white lies, which she loathed doing, but seeing Rayra was like sitting in summer sunshine; she could boost anyone's spirits. Breezy told the geese that Rayra was a designer of flea knitwear and gentlemen's cravats. Though Rayra was gifted at design, she hadn't a clue when it came to making things and, as for knitting, she'd never knitted in her life! That's why all of Breezy's scarves were made by Chatter and Banter. And cravats? Rayra liked her men rugged, not decorated!

As Edmund read *The Truth about Fish* and sipped his fifth cup of tea, Breezy nearly spilled hers at the surprise of a stripy nose pressed against the window. It was the tigress, Rayra. The oddly-matched friends embraced and whispered excitedly to one another.

'Nice place!' Rayra grinned.

'It is cosy. You look taller!'

Rayra beamed; she loved that Breezy noticed her gradual developments in height.

'Ray, do you have to peer in the window

like that? You scared me!'

'I was just curious. You make it sound like a crime to nose-in on people, Breezy,' Rayra replied cheekily.

After these pleasantries, Rayra met the geese and managed to impress Chatter — who was especially hard to please on Fridays.

'Sheesh, they're chatterboxes! I barely got a word in edgeways and you know what I'm like!' Rayra said when they were alone.

'How did you impress Chatter?'

'I took a leaf out of your book: I listened. That's all they expect, especially geese. Let's go! I want to see Ed for myself, not that I doubt your fabulous descriptions, Breez, but it's hard to believe — a troll wearing a tie?'

'Rayra, they just moved in.'

'So? They're coming for tea tomorrow and he might need some advice on how to deal with those two, I know I would!'

'He managed quite well.'

'That's why you're coming with me, I'm sure he'd love to hear it from you!'

Breezy surrendered and followed Rayra out of the house. It felt good to escape from Chatter and Banter for a bit and find out what was *really* going on outside of their theories.

A gangly troll with thin lips and bulging eyes answered the door; he bore a likeness to the fish in Edmund's book.

'Hello,' the lips mouthed blandly and coldly. He looked down his nose at Rayra, and cruelly rolled his eyes into his head when he saw Breezy clothed in burnt orange dress and a peacock blue scarf.

'We're from next door and wondered if Edmund would like to come to the next clairvoyant meeting this month,' Rayra said fearlessly.

Breezy gasped as the troll grunted and let them into the house.

The interior was unimaginative but covered in books (sadly, no fiction). There were plants and exotic herbs everywhere. Breezy couldn't fail to notice the massive walk-in fridge and wondered who had that much food to store. They were led upstairs to a white door which was ajar. Bent over a wooden desk was the tall youth. On the other side of the wall, Chatter and Banter discussed the tea party.

'Chatter, dear, why did you tell them to come in casual clothes? You know Breezy likes to dress up!'

'My dear Banter, this way we'll see

our neighbours in the clothes they're comfortable in. People behave differently in casual clothes,' Chatter replied knowingly.

'Hmm,' Banter replied with interest.

'Who're you?' Edmund said uncertainly.

Rayra grinned toothily and fluttered her eyelashes at Breezy, who tightened her grip on her insulated scarf, nervously.

'I'm your stylist for the evening.'

'What's this about?' Edmund said bluntly.

'She means, you are a very...smart person...er...troll and casual isn't in your repertoire and —' Breezy began, before Rayra interjected.

'Chatter and Banter are very particular about these things and you —'

'Dress like a fifty year old!' The phrase escaped Breezy's lips before she could stop herself.

'A good-looking fifty year old,' Rayra said reproachfully.

Breezy nodded hastily. 'But we haven't much time so —'

'We need to take you shopping,' Rayra concluded. It seemed Breezy and Rayra had adopted the geese's art of finishing each other's sentences.

The beanpole and the tigress stressed the

importance of speed in order to find the perfect outfit; Edmund gestured towards his two-seater bicycle. Realising he was serious about using it, Breezy hopped on, tucking her legs behind her. Edmund pedalled and Rayra ran in front. Breezy enjoyed feeling the wind in her hair and her scarf streaming yards behind her.

Back at the geese's, scones and iced buns were displayed on the 'tea-table', and a high chair was provided for Breezy to perch on, complete with a leg rest!

Edmund's outfit — after much evaluation — was a peacock-blue shirt with a pair of light blue jeans. Edmund had had his eye on a pair of black and grey shorts, which Rayra promptly steered him away from. The jeans suited his cyclist's figure — the two friends couldn't help but notice.

'Something's missing.' Edmund's stare cut through their feeling of a job well done.

'Oh no,' Breezy breathed, predicting his answer

'A tie.'

He was deadly serious.

'Oh lighten up, you old fogey!' Rayra replied.

'I think the peacock blue is enough to

impress the geese,' Breezy said gently.

'Are you sure?'

This question was aimed solely at Breezy, who wasn't analysing the conversation as much as Edmund, and therefore missed the hidden meaning in his overly-direct tone.

'I wouldn't have said so if I wasn't.' Breezy smiled.

'We ladies always say what we think!' Rayra said cheerily.

'Especially Chatter.' Edmund made his first joke. There was a chorus of merry laughter.

Homan achieved her goal; she hadn't eaten any snacks today. While her stomach urged her to gnaw on something, anything at all, she wondered what had gotten into Edmund. She was pleased that he was enjoying the open countryside on his bike, but he'd taken the two-seater which was most irregular for a boy like Edmund. The effects of cutting-out snacks were amazing. Homan was finally able to wear her waterproof trousers and matching tracksuit top which were only two sizes too small — she felt it was better keep things 'casual', than go over the top with anything tighter. Worried about being late, Homan didn't wait any longer for

Edmund. She wasn't worried; he'd be back before dark, he always was. Homan trudged down the path between the two houses and knocked on the door.

Edmund kept checking the time on his watch — he was trying to slow time down with his fingers and was failing. He wished he had a real keyboard that he could play to his new friends. Edmund played his keyboard while Breezy chatted with Rayra. Edmund hoped they were his friends; they rode his bicycle with him and taught him the art of conversation in preparation for the tea party. No one had ever done anything like that for him before.

***

Chatter and Banter were appalled to discover that Homan rarely drank tea and that, when she did, she added seven sugars. She was a coffee-drinker — a neurotic type according to Chatter — so they offered her what was left of the coffee Edmund had borrowed. The geese were then informed that Homan took her coffee with ten sugars — there really was no hope for the poor creature!

'What's your vocation?' Chatter shouted,

as though addressing a deaf person.

'I used to work for King Uglous —' Homan began.

'How interesting,' Banter interrupted.

'"Used to", eh? A *very* misguided lad,' Chatter squashed the first signs of smooth dialogue.

By the time Rayra and the gang reached the geese's abode, Homan had eaten a whole plate of brownies, but had drunk only four cups of coffee — she was nervous.

'Where's your husband, dear?' Chatter sensed Homan's nerves.

'He's giving a lecture,' Homan smiled weakly.

'Oh.'

'I see you have a very career orientated family!' Banter chirped.

'Yes. Edmund would flourish in the arts, but his father wishes him to be something more useful, like an astrophysicist.'

'Ridiculous! There are plenty of *those*! Banter and I worry about your son.' Chatter said.

On cue, Edmund entered the room cautiously. Eyes widened and scone-filled mouths dropped — their cake-holes hung open, literally. Edmund twinkled; it was all down to the peacock shirt. Rayra had done a good job.

'Are those jeans?' Homan stuttered. 'And that shirt is the right size! Whatever happened to saving money, Edmund?! I thought we'd agreed to wear clothes three sizes too big!'

This was why Chatter and Banter worried about Edmund, and why Edmund worried about his mother.

'So, Homan? What do you do for a living?' Rayra hoped to break the ice, and Banter gave her an encouraging nod.

'I'm a homeopath.' Homan's expression softened.

'Wow! Is that working with herbs and things?' Breezy asked enthusiastically. Edmund threw her a murderous look. But it was too late.

'*Herbs?!* Goodness, no! We don't *do* herbal - do we, Edmund?'

Edmund sat between Chatter and Homan as Breezy solemnly perched on her high chair, draping her scarf behind her. There was a long silence.

Rayra helped Banter clear the tea things — best to be careful with china when Breezy was around — and turned on the radio. Edmund received his tea successfully this time. Breezy began to tap her foot, before dancing in an unexpected manner that shocked Chatter. Yards of leg whipped through the air and Breezy's plaited hair twisted like a group of rhythmical snakes. Homan clapped and cheered, while Chatter flushed several shades of green. Rayra rolled her eyes; she was used to this. As soon as Rayra turned the radio off, Breezy resumed her perch.

'Your granddaughter feels the spirituality of the music, she's very talented!' Homan said.

'It's jazz, I'd hardly call it spiritual, but the dancing was unusual,' Edmund commented.

Chatter was chuffed. 'Well, she's *my* —'

'*Our*,' Banter corrected her.

'Yes, *our* Goosedaughter,' Chatter amended, glowing with pride.

Before Homan could embarrass herself again, Edmund spoke.

'My mother has an eye for beautiful things,' he said, looking first at his mother and then at Breezy.

'She certainly has, and must be very talented herself to bring up such a delightful and smouldering lad!' Chatter was warming up — and not just to Homan!

Rayra stifled a series of guffaws.

'Breezy is a lovely lass, as is her friend, full of vivacity,' Homan said.

'And Edmund has a lot of gumption!' Banter added.

'Too much of it sometimes,' Homan groaned.

Tactfully, Rayra, Breezy and Edmund left.

The tea party was a success. Edmund decided not to cycle around the countryside but to have another four cups of tea with Breezy instead. Rayra bid goodbye dramatically and took all of Edmund's ties with her, leaving him a new wardrobe. Despite convincing Edmund to wear jeans, Breezy couldn't part him from his beloved ties — he had a secret stash. He never became an astrophysicist, but a composer of music; he wrote the "Tea Party Suite" which was played at the Amazing Tulip's wedding.

Edmund twinkled at Breezy from afar, preferring to cycle, attend clairvoyant meetings and read *The Truth about Fish*. Breezy continued to dance alone. The following week she left Chatter and Banter's home to resume her adventures with Rayra.

The geese began gardening lessons with

Homan and christened Edmund as their 'belated Gooseson'. Jojobo began to pay more attention to his son — but sadly, his anti-social skills were so developed that he never grew out of them. That summer, the Amazing Tulip married Mr J. Long Flagpole under the watchful eyes of Chatter and Banter. Let's not forget Weather: she remained forever fickle, but became more tolerable. Gossip flowed and trolls grunted; nothing had really changed at all.

Chatter's Speculation

Chatter and Banter sat by the lake watching the ripples from Weather's touch.

'Something's afoot,' Chatter declared.

'The breeze is certainly warmer. What do you suppose has brought this change on, dear?'

'What indeed?' Chatter continued with her cross-stitch thoughtfully.

Banter waddled up and down, peering at the sky through spectacles.

'Sit down, dear!' Chatter said, exasperated. 'Whatever will the neighbours say? Besides, you're wasting your time - you'll never find the answer *up there.*'

There was a slight pause.

'You know what's happening, don't you? Why didn't you tell me?' Banter pointed at

Chatter in an accusatory manner.

'I never reveal what I know until someone mentions it first, it's common courtesy. Besides, I don't *know* dear, I *speculate,* which is as close to knowing as one can get around here,' Chatter replied.

Despite her attempt to conceal information in order to remain superior, Chatter needed the gratification of sharing knowledge with someone eager to listen, so she told Banter. Breezy hadn't visited for months and it was too early to leak her speculation to the villagers. It would soon be turned into a rumour — but not by her. She would merely suggest it to the right person.

Although Weather was omnipresent, she only saw things the way they appeared to her, at face value. Most of Arbsitchy's inhabitants were simple, comprehensible characters with two layers, whereas the minority — Chatter and Banter — had at least five identifiable layers. Weather didn't understand what she saw, but she understood feelings. Feelings determined the climate in Arbsitchy, feelings which some residents chose to deny.

Currently Weather was cloudless and saw everything clearly. A lush patch of grass on top of a hill caught her eye and she had a good feeling about it; something was about to grow!

***

Meanwhile, operating on several character levels, cunning and power-seeking Cromdork assessed the profits made from his mobile hairdressing business "Hair Today, Gone Tomorrow". Initially, the business had been exciting; travelling to new places and, most importantly, reaping profit. Soon a rota of villages to visit was established, replacing adventure with mundane routine. Customers always chose the same hairstyles, and even his employees — stylist the Blingin Sheep and windmill hairdryer The Royal Draftness — got on with their jobs without ever creating a scene in front of the customers. Cromdork detested the business. There were no power struggles; he yearned for past days when his existence consisted of reading particle pieces in his copy of *Sun-Day Space* and the *Astrophysicist's Almanac*, whilst scheming against the monarchy and women. The very thought of plots and diagrams made his elongated pupils swivel in their sockets and his lips relax until they almost formed a grin.

Cromdork banished these thoughts and fell back into the nauseous routine of watching the Blingin Sheep layering hair. The sheep's hooves drooped with the weight of his bling. Hhe looked tired, as though his creative juices had been drained. Cromdork could sympathise; he knew that it was dangerous when reserves of creativity became low, just as it was incredibly hazardous when his reserves of science-related publications became low in supply. Even the windmill felt winded. He'd started smoking to satisfy his hunger for fast food (which was unavailable in the village but had been in abundant supply at Sharson Castle) and late-night partying. His new habit was impossible to break and he started smoking inside, his propellers wafting the stale fragrance around the van, annoying some of the customers — though not enough to prevent them from attending appointments.

A less commonplace addiction consumed Miss V.O.R., ex-Royal Advisor and part-time Queen of Sharson: she loved shoes. Unlike the windmill, she dealt with her addiction; she would design her own range of shoes and open a shoe-shop and gallery for all to admire. This was a considerable change from the year before, which she spent salivating over shoes on internet shopping sites — a habit quickly passed on to Boasty Bower. Now King Uglous had grown out of his temper tantrums he did most of the ruling, giving Miss V.O.R. time to socialise with her subjects. She'd always been better with soles than with polishing the surface of things. The only dilemma she now faced was finding a location that would do her shoe-collection justice.

***

Chatter and Banter were rudely awakened by a constant humming that made their ears ring and wobbled their antique teacups.

'It must be the neighbours! They're always doing strange things in the early hours!' Chatter hissed.

'Don't do that, dear! They might send the spirits round!'

Their trollish neighbours had been in residence for a year and, despite making friends with Homan and her husband Jojobo, the gossiping geese were wary of the couple's son Edmund who liked to hold séances during the week. Chatter's feathers rippled; she was trembling, but with dignity.

'You're hysterical! Here. What would father say?' Banter poured herself and her sister a whisky from the cupboard reserved for dealing with Neighbourhood Disturbances. Wedging the glasses between their beaks (it would be indecent to swig from a bottle), they scooped up the fiery liquid, tilted their fluffy heads backwards and swallowed.

'Get the telescope!' Chatter ordered. She was ready to take action, to ensure stillness within her feathers, crockery and the village.

'Chatter!'

'What, dear?'

'It's too cloudy, we'll never be able to see anything.'

'Weather! She's hiding things from us. Banter, get your coat, we're going out.'

Weather was preoccupied. She was immersed in the rhythmic processes taking place on the same square of grass, untouched the day before. Bricks were laid, wood sawn, manual creation was happening before her eyes. It was big, it was grand, a tower fit for a god.

The geese waddled into the crisp night, their tails visible beneath the hem of their matching tweed coats like the end of a shuttlecock. Their feathers were ruffled and they were determined to discover the source of the humming. They followed a trail of pink fairy lights up the hill.

The geese halted in front of a small boutique; they pressed their beaks up against the windows and peered inside. They saw a tousled brown head full of ribbons, scraps of velvet and…glitter. Caught working late into the night, Miss V.O.R. became flustered; designing shoes had transformed into an unhealthy obsession.

'What in Weather's name are you up to, young lady?' Chatter rose to her full height, returning to her past role as Headmistress of the village school.

'Creating such a disturbance at this time of night,' Banter flapped, without missing a beat.

'Cluttering up the neighbourhood with… What premises are you running anyway?'

'A shoe shop,' Miss V.O.R. breathed guiltily.

'Oh…' Chatter squawked.

'Well…' Banter fluttered.

'Mind if we take a look?' Chatter forced her way onto the chaotic threshold.

'What's your name, dear?' Banter hovered, intent on questioning the hemmed-in designer.

'Stiletta, but I'm more commonly known as V.O.R.'

'V.O.R.?' Chatter bent down to inspect the suspicious glamour, resulting in a muffled voice and bottom-up effect.

'Miss V.O.R?' The name was familiar to Banter. She suddenly felt guilty about imposing her presence on the lady.

'As in Voice of Reason?' Chatter was now upright, facing Miss V.O.R. The tables had turned.

'That's right,' Stiletta replied, eager to repair a wandering sole.

'I see,' the geese chorused, sharing a bemused glance.

'What's that?' Banter returned to her role of interrogator.

'My sewing machine. It's the Hummingbird 1000, the very latest model. See how small the stitches are? One thousand stitches per minute.' Stilletta's eyes glistened, her voice filled with pride.

'Did you say *hummingbird*?'

'Yes, she did.' Chatter responded for The Voice of Reason, who'd lost her voice in the depths of the new machine.

'I'd no idea it would make that much noise,' Miss V.O.R. blushed.

'We hear everything,' Chatter said.

'We're very light sleepers,' Banter added.

'Maybe there's a fault in the machine...' Stilletta replied, feeling unravelled. She stroked the machine lovingly and peered at the motor.

'You'll have to cut your stitches down, dear.'

'Do it by hand,' Chatter chipped in.

'Stitch to a two four rhythm, it's always lulled me to sleep...'

'Modern technology, the curse of the earth,' Chatter hissed.

'Goodnight dear!' Banter honked pleasantly.

'Have a pleasant and *quiet* night!' Chatter squawked shrilly.

The sisters goose-swaggered in perfect unison as they exited the boutique, leaving Stilletta feeling frayed.

Once outside, Banter turned to Chatter. 'Do you really think that machine could make as much noise as that?'

'Of course not! Don't be ridiculous, dear. But one must put one's foot down and show them who rules the roost.'

'I agree.'

They swaggered homewards.

Behind the geese was a swirling mist; Weather had decided to hide this area from them until she knew more herself.

It rained that night. Weather felt embarrassed. She'd been crying and everyone in Sharson would know when they saw the wet ground. Her tears started as a snivelling drizzle before turning into large droplets that fell thick and fast, forming puddles. The watery stuttering and howling noises she made caused her to cloud over with shame. The worst part was that she didn't know why she was crying. No one had upset her. Her previous downpour had been when Edmund the Evaluator attempted to forecast her, as though *she* had predictable behavioural patterns like the people of Sharson! It was a violation of the right to remain mysterious and a woman's prerogative to change her mind. She wasn't sure why she had wept so, but for some reason Weather didn't feel so hot. Perhaps she was picking up on the feeling of disappointment wafting through Sharson.

One inhabitant who was feeling content was award-winning Russian Chef, Furnace

Clatterpot. He was famous for his exquisite flavours and small portions, making his customers desire more until they became dependent on consuming his dishes and no one else's. As small in stature as his portions, he made up for his lack of height with his volatile and fiery attitude in the kitchen. Furnace was very particular about his kitchen; he sterilised all crockery with vodka. Today he would sterilise his new restaurant with the help of his waitress and henchwoman, the Bandylegged Banshee. The waitress, commonly known as Bandylegs, was chosen by Clatterpot for her shrill voice. Currently she was eating a lollipop, while Furnace rushed around spraying vodka on the bricks of his soon-to-be restaurant from an extinguished fire-extinguisher.

Seeing this, Weather felt sorry for the little man and decided to summon a slight breeze to help spread the steriliser, followed by scorching sunshine to dry the area. This kind deed made her feel better and the sunshine absorbed her tears from the night before, saving her the embarrassment of her behaviour becoming village gossip.

***

An unfortunate incident was about to occur in "Hair Today, Gone Tomorrow". The Regurgitator — a domestic rat — had recently discovered the mobile hairdressing business when it stopped outside the Town Hall where he lived. He was a creature who latched onto the thoughts of others, only to repeat them later. In previous years, the Town Hall had been the centre of the community, flowing with gossip for him to propel into the ears of passers-by. It was something he looked forward to. When events at the Town Hall ceased and the building fell into decline, he felt lost.

That was before he discovered the mobile hairdressers. There was something about the stylist there that made the customers spill their secrets. Then there was the goose sisters who revealed seeds of information to each other, just waiting to be sown. If he chose his position carefully, he could tune in and absorb each utterance, whilst having the hair around his ears trimmed at the same time for optimum auditory clarity.

It had been a quiet day. The Blingin Sheep settled down with a copy of *Cornish Coiffeurs* and the Royal Draftness lit a cigarette.

Cromdork was also enjoying the stillness. It gave him time to ponder the exact number of degrees required for each angled cut — the asymmetric styles proved quite a challenge to calculate. The insistent tap of platform boots caused an irritated Cromdork to raise an eyebrow. The Blingin Sheep eyed the new customer's head and shoulders, before glancing at her bony, inwardly inclined legs.

'I'd like a bob,' the Bandylegged banshee giggled, leaning towards the stylist in an intimidating fashion.

'Are we talking Keira Knightley or Twiggy?' the sheep bleated, filing his nails.

'Keira of course! Except mine will be prettier than *hers,* obviously.' The pigeon-toed predator flung her hair over her shoulder and tottered towards a chair.

The sheep noticed that Cromdork had left his corner. The particle-loving manager was on his feet, helping their most critical, yet faithful customers, Chatter and Banter, into chairs. Pre-occupied by the influx of customers, no one noticed a scurrying shape settle at the base of the windmill hair-dryer.

The Blingin Sheep felt relieved when it was time for the Royal Draftness to dry the banshee's hair. She'd pouted and fluttered her mascara-laden lashes at him for an hour whilst lecturing him on vegetarianism, oblivious to the fact that he himself was a sheep and understood it full well.

Cromdork felt extremely uncomfortable next to Chatter and Banter and his right eye had begun to twitch. The last time he'd entertained the geese while they waited for their weekly perm was dreadful. They'd attempted to peck his cheek! Not in anger, but in the form of a friendly kiss — which was much worse! They'd cornered him, a goose on each side; he couldn't wait until the high-pitched customer's hair was done so he could escape.

The Universe responded to Cromdork's plight. There was a foul-mouthed exclamation from the Royal Draftness, followed by the sound of scurrying and the glimpse of a pink tail. The windmill dropped his cigarette in shock and it plummeted downwards onto the freshly bobbed head of the Bandylegged customer. Chatter and Banter swooped in, flapping and honking as only anxious geese can. The flames rose, creating a vicious Mohican.

The banshee jumped in the air, her legs straightening momentarily, before returning to their crooked stance.

She let out a hair-raising scream before shouting at them all. 'My hair! You've burned the roots, it'll never be as luscious as before. You've killed a living organism! Murderers!'

She proceeded by wagging a chewed fingernail stump in the Blingin Sheep's face and rose to her full height — which was an inch higher from when she was seated — and all the while flames frolicked on top of her head. Still cooking, she glared at Cromdork, who'd escaped from the geese in the heat of the moment and now watched from a safe distance whilst eating a can of tuna.

'Meat is murder!' she roared, in decibels undiscovered.

'Actually, it's fish,' the manager replied.

On her way out she turned to the geese. 'Ladies, thank you for your assistance, feel free to come to my friend's restaurant opening, you'll be welcome. The rest of you pigs will be turned away!' She flicked her head, sending embers flying and causing the door frame to catch alight.

True to its name, the mobile's customer had had *hair today*, which would definitely be *gone tomorrow*.

This time, the geese didn't flap but calmly

helped the windmill, the sheep and the scientist to smother the flames. Sadly, three quarters of the mobile was reduced to ashes.

***

Although "Hair Today Gone Tomorrow" had been cut, another business was forged from passion. The structure on the hill was complete. Inside, Furnace Clatterpot lovingly removed a Lemon Meringue pie from the oven and paused to look out of the window; the sun shone and the birds sang. He smiled grimly and sighed. Bandylegs' dark eyes were firmly focused on the dessert and she pouted earnestly, resisting temptation. Furnace used thick lard in his desserts, an animal product which she, as a dedicated vegetarian, refused to eat. As the sugary sweetness drifted into her barrelled nostrils, she gripped the table and her bandy legs juddered violently.

Weather peeked through a passing cloud, watching the whole scene. She was in awe of the chef's creations; there were already ten desserts lined up on the worktop. Instead of distributing her warmth across Arbsitchy, she stayed where she was.

***

Chatter couldn't keep still. Her feathers rippled hysterically and her eyes darted manically as she glared out of the window.

'Who was it?!'

'What, dear?' Banter, bespectacled, looked up from her knitting.

'Who *dared* to encroach upon *our* territory?' Chatter's webbed foot came down, like a fly swatter.

'How about some tea, dear?' Banter soothed.

'I *should* know! Why don't I know?!'

'I'm afraid, I haven't the foggiest. Perhaps we should ask the neighbours?'

'We should know, we know everything! We are — were — the village gospel!' Chatter's beady eyes softened and glistened as her tail drooped sorrowfully. Banter had never seen her sister like this.

'I thought you said we speculate?'

'I don't know about you, my dear, but I just *know* things! Perhaps we're too old for this. Soon they'll want some young thing to tell them the goings-on, instead of us!' Chatter blew her beak on a pink handkerchief.

'Don't say that. No one would be able to follow in our goose steps. We're pillars of the community!' Banter's words lingered, mingling with the scent of Earl Grey. Suddenly, she set down her knitting and waddled over to Chatter. 'I smell a rat, dear.'

This disturbance had, in fact, been caused by a rat known as The Regurgitator, who had been present on the day of the fire and had spread the news as rapidly. His style of gossiping was different to Chatter's and Banter's. Chatter and Banter were laid-back, whereas The Regurgitator was desperate to get the words out, feeling calm once he had revealed all, before his mouth watered for more gossip.

Things for Chatter and Banter were about to go "bottoms up". Instead of tramping next door to *hear* the news, Homan and Jojobo were impudent enough to *tell* the geese the news. Desperate, Chatter and Banter started to regularly patrol the village, as they had to make their presence felt. However, the Regurgitator wasn't their only rival. The village was evolving into a complex place. Consumed by their grief and wallowing in a state of unknowing, the geese failed to notice that Weather had been shining and spreading warmth for too long; the balance of things would soon be destroyed.

***

Despite attempts to advertise the restaurant, business was quiet for Furnace. He was so desperate for custom that he decided to offer free vodka to anyone who came. So far, he was the only one consuming the vodka. Somewhere between his second and third bottle — and Bandylegs' seventh monologue on the sin of meat-eating — Furnace realised that all they needed was a landmark to let people know where they were. The food was the least of his worries; he had a magical culinary touch.

Meanwhile, Stilletta's creativity wasn't well-trained. It came in bursts and took over, leaving her exhausted when her masterpieces were complete. She'd been sleeping in her shop, using leather for a blanket and a shoebox for a pillow. After weeks of this routine, the ex-advisor took her own advice and resolved to go for regular walks in her designs.

Cromdork and the gang were also spending time outdoors. Used to being mobile, they travelled during the day and camped in tents at night. All had adapted well to exposure to the elements... Well, all except for Cromdork, who had waged a vendetta against the whole of the insect race. He'd created a radar system to track the beasts and a contraption similar to a Venus flytrap to kill them. The Blingin Sheep didn't complain but found that excess exposure to the elements ruined his bling and his hair. However, The Royal Draftness was in his element. He'd missed the simple existence of responding to natural wind, rather than generating his own.

All three had been quiet since the fire. Each felt the business had lost its shine and each wanted to return to his roots. This desire wasn't expressed but was instinctively known amongst the three, who soon separated. The Royal Draftness left to find a nice, windy spot and the Blingin Sheep bought a one-way ticket to Paris to embark on the ambitious feat of Poodle Hair Design. Cromdork, who only really thought ahead when scheming, had noticed that his shoes would only last another forty-two hours before the stitching completely fell apart and geared himself up to go shopping. This was an act that held the risk of bumping into females, but sturdy shoes were essential before he could take the necessary steps to finding a new vocation. Despite being an astrophysicist, Cromdork still found comfort in gravity and having his feet on the ground.

Furnace Clatterpot had made twenty-five desserts, forty salads and been to the market twice. The chef hadn't found a landmark for his restaurant and he couldn't use Bandylegs as a representative; not only was she too thin to advertise good food, she was irritating. While Furnace sang in low crescendos, Bandylegs painted her nails a sickly shade of magenta using "animal friendly" varnish. As she admired the reflection of her bottom in a mixing bowl, she knocked over the nail polish, sending the gloopy liquid straight into the soufflés, staining them mauve. Furnace's eyes flashed. Grabbing the meat cleaver, he chased her out of the kitchen, the vain banshee wailing as she fled. Furnace returned, as deflated as his soufflés. Weather saw him hunched over the sink, crying, and vowed to help.

***

After the success of his version of the fire, the Regurgitator felt rejuvenated. He scurried around feverishly, enhancing his eavesdropping skills. Before long he could hear the gossip in the neighbouring villages and tune into multiple conversations at once. His ratty face now had a manic expression and his ears were twice their original size.

Cromdork's existing shoes were shrinking in size. He'd almost lost his sole. He walked with purpose. His knowledge of geography, physics and profit-making told him that the best location for a shoe shop would be on top of a hill. The reasoning behind this being that by the time one reached the top, their shoes would be worn out and the climb down would contribute to wearing the new pair out. Arbsitchy terrain was infamous for its molehills, manholes and troll prints; one never knew where they or their shoes would end up! The scientist was right, but Stilletta hadn't chosen her shop's location on the basis of terrain — she just liked the view from the hilltop. Cromdork hadn't come across many of the female species and his trachea tightened when he saw the shop window lined with purple glitter. The glitter brought back memories of Herpursurly — a woman who loved purple along with anything paint-splattered. He gritted his teeth and entered.

Cromdork's worries were confirmed when he saw a flustered female hunched over a sewing machine.

'Hello,' the female said. She had a colony of buttons and fabric nesting in her hair.

Not another artist, Cromdork thought.

'I require a pair of shoes, black, without laces, made from Italian leather.' He scanned the messy workshop.

'Um...hold on a sec.' The female delved into the detritus, emerging quite unexpectedly next to Cromdork.

'I haven't any men's shoes in stock, I'm afraid. If you come back two hours I'll have a pair ready for you.'

'I'd prefer to stay here and observe the work, if you don't mind.' It was a statement rather than a question.

Stiletta recognised the customer from his tone of voice as Cromdork, the man who'd attempted to seize the Sharson throne. She found a rickety chair for him to sit on.

His close surveillance unnerved her, but she soon became absorbed in creating a pair of shoes to suit the schemer's feet. She was thrilled to be working on a different type of footwear. The design was sketched and approved within five minutes, and the shoes completed in less than two hours — which was lucky, as Cromdork had been counting the seconds.

Cromdork raised an eyebrow when he saw his new shoes. They were unexpected, intriguing to say the least and there was nothing he could find fault with. They were exactly what he'd asked for, yet somehow different; they were somewhat fashionable.

'What do you think?' the designer asked, chewing her hair anxiously.

'Most acceptable.' Cromdork shook her hand, paid the agreed amount and left.

Stiletta realised she'd achieved the impossible. She'd combined art with practicality in one design. This would inspire her new range of shoes.

***

The air buzzed with electrical energy; Weather was excited. She felt connected to the chef as his temperament was similar to hers. Most of the villagers were overcast when it came to feelings, so Weather admired Furnace's ability to express his.

She glowed and this glow spread to the hilltop, illuminating The Royal Draftness. Her plan was in place. Furnace would notice the windmill in no time due to the din The Royal Draftness was making and the light bouncing off his propellers. However, Furnace was oblivious to 'goings-on' beyond his kitchen and it took time for the chef to notice Weather's sign, more time than she'd anticipated.

Several hours passed and The Royal Draftness continued to rap. By the time Furnace noticed the windmill, Weather was asleep. Meat cleaver and vodka in hand, the award-winning chef staggered into the night. Bandylegs remained in the kitchen, intensely focused on her reflection in the saucepans. After several layers of animal-friendly makeup had been applied to her face, she took a walk.

Furnace felt insecure because he was no longer the only masculine figure on the hill. The windmill's bravado-filled sway alarmed him; he needed to reinstate his masculinity. Furnace brandished his meat cleaver and growled in Russian. The windmill grunted in response. They say actions speak louder than words but, for both males, both words and actions proved to be more productive.

'Who are you?' the chef asked haughtily.

'Who are *you*?' the windmill grunted.

'An award-winning Chef, known to women worldwide for my melt-in-the-mouth Pavlova.' Furnace stood his ground.

'I am — *was* — Royal Windmill to King Uglous and am infamous for late-night partying and farting.' The Royal Draftness swayed.

'Ah. Vodka?'

'Vodka!'

Suddenly there was a feeling of mutual respect for each other's lifestyles. Furnace dropped his cleaver. The men embraced. After many toasts, the windmill was asked to be the restaurant's landmark.

After that, Weather's first gift to Furnace was the crisp, blanket of snow. She was in love.

***

Cromdork was also taking a walk and, unbeknownst to him, was being tailed by the Regurgitator. The rat had been peering into Stilletta's shop — he loved looking at women's shoes — when he saw the scientist emerge, altered. His ears tingled; surely some deep secret was about to be revealed.

Cromdork felt strangely connected to the Earth, significantly more than ever before. His head was free from thoughts of quarks, cosmic fluff, black holes and other equalling absorbing matter. His mind was also free of dark matter and dark matters such as scheming. With each Italian leather cushioned footfall, his astronomical aspirations diminished.

Cromdork analysed his life; his scheme to seize the throne had had political undertones and a desire to oversee for the greater good, as had the hairdressing business which had been an asset to the community. Deep down the scientist was a politician. He didn't just care about the universe, he was beginning to care about the people in it. This realisation was a small step for Cromdork but would be a giant leap for Arbsitchy.

For scientists, theories must be proven, but for Chatter and Banter, merely theorising was adequate. For the Regurgitator, any snippet of information was gospel. Cromdork often thought aloud — that was why the universe was so in tune with him. However, on this occasion this meant that he wouldn't have time to test his theory before making his all-important career decision, for as soon as the Regurgitator overheard Cromdork say 'beadle', he scampered off. He didn't know what a 'beadle' was, but he had to spread the word.

Within an hour, the word had been spread to Bandylegs on her way back from Stiletta's boutique. The rat had chosen his messenger wisely as the Banshee's voice was loud enough for both Arbsitchy and the neighbouring villages to hear.

Cromdork puffed out his chest, posing for photographs. It was so *easy*. Grant a few favours and all of a sudden you become a respected figure! Mr J. Long Flagpole had *noticed* Cromdork. The Regurgitator's messages had, in this instance, aided someone; Cromdork's utterance of the title 'beadle' had been passed on to each resident, until this idea became the truth. The first thing the scientist had done as 'beadle' was greet the residents of Arbsitchy. He'd never been good at small-talk, but discovered that Weather was always a successful topic of conversation.

***

During her walk — or rather, totter — Bandylegs discovered the shoe shop. After rigorous hair flicking (she'd had hair extensions put in after the fire), strutting and mirror-squinting, she'd made her decision. However, Stiletta had fallen asleep.

'Wake UP!' the banshee bellowed. 'I *have* to have these.'

Too tired to reprimand the banshee's impatience, Stiletta examined the pair in question. They were stripy platforms — not at all suitable for Bandylegs' waitressing duties. Stiletta dutifully packaged the shoes and kissed them goodbye.

Bandylegs tore open the tissue paper and forced the shoes on. Outside it was snowing. Bandylegs seemed reluctant to pay. She chewed her nails nervously, before the pile of sandwich packets in the bin caught her eye and she smiled.

'Do you know how many calories are in those things?'

Stiletta blushed in response to Bandlegs' observation.

'I can see that you're a working woman, but *really*, you should look after yourself. I could bring you the best food you've ever

tasted for a week as payment for the shoes.'
Bandylegs fluttered her powdered eyelids.

'It *would* be handy to have some help,'
Stiletta smiled. Bandylegs flicked her hair in
response and marched into the snow.

Stiletta was pleased, but couldn't help
feeling bad that the shoes' first walk was in
the snow where no one could see them. She
hoped that they would be well-cared for, but
was doubtful.

***

Chatter and Banter had theorised that
the person responsible for leaking the
news about the mobile hairdressers was
an outsider and unlikely to threaten their
position again. As they were tolerant
individuals, they would shake the whole
thing off. After a refreshing swim, they were
back on schedule, ready to patrol outside of
their normal jurisdiction.

'We must go up the hill, dear,' Chatter
said.

'What a splendid notion, sister!' Banter
cried, clasping her wings together.

'I want to know what that lady with the
shop is up to,' Chatter said.

150

'She's hardly a lady with all those ribbons in her hair, she's almost as dishevelled as Weather!' Banter added.

'Quite right! What about the new restaurant? I wonder if they do cream tea,' Chatter gabbled excitedly.

'Cream tea will do my nerves the world of good.'

The geese chuckled and, grabbing their parasols, strolled out of their front gate.

***

Bandylegs tottered into the boutique carrying, rather precariously, a tray of goat's cheese and red onion tart, fresh fruit salad and a glass of homemade lemonade. Stiletta looked up on hearing the clacking of shoes across the floorboards. She noticed that her creation had survived so far.

'Thanks for the food.'

'It's nothing, darling. Thanks for the shoes, they're adorable! If you like the food, you can have the meals all year round.'

'What will that cost?'

'Several pairs of shoes, of course.'

'What about payment for the chef?'

'What he doesn't know won't hurt him.

All he's after is a few compliments; if you don't rave about the food, he goes berserk! But don't worry, I've brought you some sheets to write your comments on.'

The fashion-conscious banshee chatted for an hour, before pausing to look at her watch.

'Look at the time! It's my lunch break.' With a meaningful squint at the shoes waiting to go in the window display, she left.

***

Chatter and Banter were polishing off their cream tea in a most dignified manner.

'That really was most exquisite, wasn't it dear?' Chatter said.

'Absolute heaven,' Banter replied.

'We won't tell the chef, of course.' Chatter stared pointedly at her sister.

'Of course not! He'd only get comfortable and wouldn't put so much effort into producing the food.'

'Compliments result in comfort and comfort results in laziness,' Chatter added superiorly.

'I couldn't agree more!'

At that moment, Bandylegs sat down

opposite the geese, smoothing her hair. She was oblivious to the flames and shouts coming from the kitchen. Crowds of people had seen The Royal Draftness' trademark sway and had come to the restaurant.

'Good afternoon, ladies,' the waitress inclined her head. Interestingly, her hair didn't move with her head; in fact, it didn't move at all, except for when she flicked it.

'Good afternoon,' the geese chorused icily.

Chatter looked down her beak at the waitress. Bandylegs wasn't fazed and continued to speak.

'Don't you think this village is still in like…the Stone Age?' Bandylegs pouted.

Chatter snorted.

'That's why this ceremony with Mr J. Long Flagpole is *so* important!' the waitress continued.

'What ceremony?' the geese enquired.

'Why… I thought you two fine ladies knew? The ceremony to introduce a beadle for the protection of the village. He's a bit gloomy-looking I must say, but he has some interesting prospects lined up for the future of Arbsitchy. My furry friend, Gurgy, or the Regurgitator as he calls himself, told me. I truly feel that rats are underestimated. He lost his family to medical experimentation, you know.' Bandylegs raised her voice as though performing to a vast audience. After which, she gulped some air and continued.

'Of course, if it wasn't for Furnace, I'd be right down there with all the others watching this historic moment, but he needs me; I'm his sunshine, you see. It's a shame, though, as I just love to look at Mr J. Long Flagpole. It's so dreamy the way he towers close to the clouds! Such a shame he's now married.' She sighed and clomped into kitchen.

The geese were upset. As the eldest residents, *they* were the village's past, present and future. They weren't about to surrender their position to some upstart! The wellbeing of Arbsitchy was their domain. They didn't feel threatened — after all, who could *ever* do as much for Arbsitchy as they had done? And who knew the residents better than they did? They merely felt wronged, which was considerably worse than feeling threatened.

The sisters didn't say anything. Each knew the other's thoughts, and so they set down their teacups and left without filling in the comments sheet. Furnace chased after them, desperate for a compliment, but the geese waddled on; they were on a mission. The frustrated chef marched back into the restaurant with all the masculinity he could muster. In an attempt to detract his attention from the ungracious geese, Weather shone her brightest and melted the snow, leaving sparkling pools of water.

The geese were in need of reassurance and it was essential they reassert their authority. Their destination was the shoe boutique. Both knew they could count on the designer to be appropriately dishevelled with enough material for them to find fault with.

The boutique door jangled. A neatly combed head looked up.

'Can I help you?' Stiletta smiled.

Chatter glanced at the bin; it was empty. Shoes lined the walls neatly, a material cupboard had been put in and the only visible detritus was that which the designer was currently working on. Stiletta looked happy and well-fed, quite different to the flustered and anxious woman the geese had first encountered.

'Everything seems to be in order.' Chatter raised an eyebrow at her sister. Finally, both fluffed their feathers and waddled out of the shop.

Stiletta exhaled, smiled and began to stitch with steady purpose.

Chatter and Banter were the only residents not at home and were blind to what was unfolding before their eyes.

'Natural order has been disturbed, sister!' Banter sniffed, flapping her wings erratically.

'Feel free to blame it on Mother Nature, dear. I blame human nature,' Chatter paused for effect, her eyes darting this way and that, before continuing in a low voice; 'It's a conspiracy, I tell you!'

***

For once, Chatter was wrong. Weather was a powerful influence on the mood of the village and she was exhausted. She'd shone for a fortnight and kept the clouds to the consistency of Furnace's Meringues, but it had all been in vain; she hadn't managed to whisk the chef away from the restaurant. He'd ventured outside once to test his recipes out on The Royal Draftness — who responded with appreciative burps — but the chef never acknowledged the sky.

While Weather stewed, Furnace was about to bubble over with red-hot fury because he hadn't received any compliments from his customers. He was desperate and had started handing out roses to female customers but Bandylegs was the one who profited from this, as she gave the roses to male customers and received more compliments than the chef! The villagers weren't open about their feelings and, though the chef had met their standards of fine cuisine, they'd yet to give him the response he deserved.

Cromdork hadn't visited the restaurant; he was a busy beadle and was working on his figure. He was particularly worried about his 'overhang' — the area of his tummy which hung over his trousers — which was, in his opinion, moving lower by the minute due to gravitational pull and the lack of friction in his life.

Bandylegs caused friction wherever she went. As far as she was concerned, Furnace was nothing without her. After all, she delivered the food and the delivery was extremely important. You had to make people feel special. This was why she violently batted her eyelashes at customers and made a fuss of them, before neglecting them when the next customer arrived. After she carried out the initial serving, the customers had to work for her attention. She'd decided to leave Arbsitchy but she hadn't told Furnace, it would only upset him. She needed an excuse to leave for a little while – but Furnace wasn't aware of her plan.

***

Stiletta had been working rapidly. Weather's constant shine kept the sky light for more hours than usual and the Shoe Designer took advantage of this to continue working. When she heard from a certain rat that Cromdork had been appointed Beadle, she couldn't help but soften with pride as it was her design that had repaired his wandering sole.

Stiletta's sole problem was that her creative muscles weren't being built up properly. Bandylegs brought her vegetarian meals in exchange for muscle-building heels, but the designer felt stitched up and was in desperate need of protein. She would confront the waitress about it and politely ask for a more diverse selection of dishes, as there was only so much blue cheese, salad and Quorn she could endure.

Breakfast hadn't seemed an appropriate time to make demands, so the designer waited until lunchtime to speak to Bandylegs. She knew that whatever she said she'd have to be immensely tactful.

'Thanks, I really appreciate your efforts. You must be tired after rushing around in those platforms all morning, have a seat.' Stiletta took the tray of food offered by Bandylegs.

'Thanks hun, but I don't sit,' the waitress stated. 'It flattens my bottom out too much and I'm trying to keep it pert. It's nearly my lunch break so I can't stay long,' Bandylegs continued, eager to totter off.

Stiletta spoke rapidly as she knew that once the waitress started talking, there was no hope of her being heard. 'I've a comment to make about the food. It melts in my mouth and every bite is spiritually replenishing, however it lacks… Well, meat. It's like me selling you the shoe without its heel. Perhaps, a mixture of vegetarian and meat dishes could be brought?'

It began with a twitch of the mouth, which developed into a frown, then eventually escalated until the banshee was pointing her finger. Bandylegs had found her reason to leave the restaurant.

'You make me sick! You make shoes out of leather, animals are suffering to satisfy your needs and you are ungracious! It's against my ethics to serve the boiled, dead flesh of innocent animals! I quit!'

The truth was that Bandylegs didn't have the time or energy to give a long spiel, so she only made a brief dig at the meat-eating population. She finished by discarding the platform shoes and stomping off, before running back to enquire whether any part of the shoe was made from leather. As the shoes were made from wood and plastic she snatched them, before leaving Arbsitchy for good.

***

Furnace's compliment sheets became complex, ten-paged forms that had to be completed otherwise the bill wasn't brought and the customers couldn't leave. The customers couldn't please Furnace and neither could Weather. Glorious Mediterranean sunshine was now expected of her to bring customers into the restaurant. The clouds were beginning to step out of line and, although she was being consistent, Furnace leapt about chasing people with his meat cleaver regularly. Neither was there peace at night — Furnace only slept soundly when there was a slight breeze in the air combined with a thick mist, so he had trouble sleeping most of the time.

It wasn't easy to generate a light breeze combined with thick mist. Weather gave up. It began to rain.

***

As a Natural Scientist, Cromdork was constantly aware of the weather conditions — he refused to refer to weather as a person. He liked changeable weather but loathed long periods of sunshine or cold, as they made him cranky. He disliked the universe following a constant pattern as it didn't cater to his enjoyment of explosions and investigation. If everything was known and there were no sudden changes in life, there wouldn't be a need for scientific theories. In short, if everything were known, life would be dull.

The weather irked Cromdork. It was too hot. Sunshine brought insects, unnecessary cheerfulness and hurt his eyes. He had a bad feeling about Weather — he winced at his reference to her as a person — because she was a woman and there was no telling what she'd do! He would contact Edmund.

Edmund the Evaluator was Cromdork's longest friend at primary school. Cromdork would scheme and relay his plan to Edmund who would approve the plan by responding with 'right.' He was contacted that evening. Edmund was, in truth, glad of the opportunity to get away from university, as he found his course on 'the Behavioural Patterns of Goldfish' rather predictable. Despite managing to maintain a balanced a schedule of work and leisure, he'd noticed that his bike rides became longer. A need to feel challenged and surprised clouded his habitually neutral aura; even the spirits at the Student Clairvoyance Meeting had told him that his evaluation skills weren't being fully exploited. He immediately saddled his bicycle — complete with its emergency picnic basket — and set off.

***

Within a week of Cromdork's beadle

ceremony, the geese had drunk the contents of their cupboard for Neighbourhood Disturbances. They no longer took walks but bitterly speculated about Cromdork's character. They were surprised to see their gooseson at their gate.

'Quick, Banter! The bottles!'

'Where should I put them?' Banter fluttered.

'Hide them in the oven,' Chatter commanded, 'and remove your curlers, you look most common!'

'Hello, Edmund dear. We weren't expecting you at all, were we, Banter?'

'Not at all, you'll have to excuse our nightdresses, they're terribly worn.'

'Right,' their gooseson said.

'Do sit down!' Banter urged.

'You haven't been around any spirits, have you?' Edmund scoured the shadowy corners of the room.

Chatter and Banter looked at one another and at the Neighbourhood Disturbances cupboard.

'None,' Banter squeaked.

'There are no disturbed presences in the house?'

'None,' Chatter responded.

'Right.' He sounded disappointed; he'd missed the séances he'd held next door.

'Why don't you have a cup of tea, dear, and tell us why you're here,' Banter said.

The geese were shocked and angry to hear that Edmund had been summoned to Arbsitchy by the beadle and that Edmund knew more about Weather's troubles than they did. Edmund would stay for a month to observe Weather.

Had she known that she was being observed, Weather would've played a trick on Edmund. However, her spirits were too low to joke around. The rain was constant and fell in heavy sheets. This was sorrow; blind fury had not reached her yet.

Cromdork visited each villager, brandishing leaflets he'd designed explaining how one should act in an emergency. He'd even included diagrams. He found it difficult not to explain the situation in terms of physics; however, the finished leaflets contained language designed to cushion any panic arising from the words 'danger' or 'emergency.' Cromdork also explained Edmund's presence in the village. Chatter and Banter were the last villagers on his list. They gave the beadle any icy reception.

'Freak weather? Floods? Hurricanes? It'll never happen.' The geese slammed the door in Cromdork's face.

After careful observation, evaluation and colossal amounts of tea, Edmund reached his verdict. The Regurgitator was hiding in a bush waiting to relay the message, while Stiletta cut ribbon to calm her anxiety.

'If my analysis is correct, there'll be storms and freak weather. You'll need an expert on site. I can't predict exactly what will occur and neither can the spirits I consulted.'

'An expert?' Cromdork queried.

'Right.' Edmund straightened his waterproof tie.

'Do you know anyone?' Cromdork attempted to draw further information out of the troll.

'No. I don't mix with anyone outside of my study.' He mounted his bicycle.

'I do!' Stiletta leapt up, showering them with ribbons.

'*You*?' Cromdork sneered.

'Ernest Tremor, he used to assess Sharson Castle and take steps to strengthen the wall.' Stiletta produced Ernest Tremor's business card from inside her pink diary. 'I made him

165

a pair of disaster-proof boots recently,' she added. The Regurgitator wrote this down.

'Thank you,' Cromdork responded coldly, but courteously.

Ernest Tremor proved tricky to track down. Being of a nervous disposition, the natural disaster expert didn't stay in one place for long.

***

Arbsitchy had been struck with layers of a stubborn type of frost that mercilessly found its way into every corner of the village. Mr J. Long Flagpole was laced with threads of ice that curled around him like weeds, slowly freezing the life out of him. His wife, the Amazing Tulip, had moved to a greenhouse as she was in danger of catching frost bite and snapping. Chatter and Banter continued to deny Weather's dangerous condition. The ubiquitous and dishevelled woman's heart had turned to a block of ice, and this was only the tip of the iceberg. A scorned woman was a formula for disaster. Weather's hurt clouded her vision; she was oblivious to those who really mattered.

The geese ignored Weather and continued

to patrol, skating across the ice nonchalantly. Cromdork visited the residents regularly, checking that they were comfortable.

Icy gusts of wind circled the village, Weather howled until another sound, more menacing, reverberated through Arbsitchy. The ice was melting; the village began to flood.

Several years ago, half of the houses in Arbsitchy had been rebuilt; the other half, however, remained the same as the builder had a short attention span and easily became bored. This meant that several houses from the 16th century hadn't been restored and were in danger of collapsing. One of these houses belonged to Chatter and Banter.

Where was award winning chef, Furnace Clatterpot, at this moment? He was dicing vegetables. His main worry was what to do when he ran out of things to chop. He worried about dying so early on in his career - what if there was a better chef out there? He contemplated this for a moment, before reassuring himself that he was still the best. His compliment sheets kept him going and he intended to survive.

***

Cromdork paced back and forth, thinking. He knew that soon he'd have to swim into the village to break the news to the geese that their only chance for survival would be to shelter inside The Royal Draftness. The scientist hoped that if everything turned out well, he would at least receive an outfit to go with his position — hopefully one that would hide his overhang. Just as thoughts of his overhang began to trouble him, he heard someone cough. He turned to see a small, round man with soft, round features and curly blonde hair.

'Mr. Tremor, I presume?' Cromdork shook the small man's soft hand.

'Qu-quite r-right. W-where's the disaster?' Mr. Tremor tried to control his trembling.

'She's everywhere, but before we get to that, there's another *situation* that needs dealing with.'

'What sort of situation?' The small man trembled.

'It involves *females* — two actually — who are — how should I express this? Avalanches embodied. You'll need to be careful — maybe even wear protective clothing,' Cromdork said.

As the scientist explained the situation of Chatter and Banter's vulnerable residence, the natural disaster expert grew taller, ceased to shake and looked serenely powerful.

'I'll take care of it.' He tipped his bowler hat at Cromdork, straightened his trouser brace and left.

Cromdork resumed caring for the residents of Arbsitchy. He advised all those without a sturdy home to assemble on the hill and make their way inside the windmill — who'd kindly offered to rap to take their mind off Weather. For The Royal Draftness it was like attending a late-night party except that, instead of thumping music, the heavens were banging and crashing. Cromdork enjoyed the uncertainty of it all; he wondered whether the world was scheduled to end, but then decided to focus on the pleasant explosive sounds from above instead.

The Regurgitator, Cromdork, Stiletta and Chatter and Banter — if they surrendered — would shelter inside the windmill. Furnace had been asked to join them but he was too proud, preferring to remain in his kitchen. Stiletta and the Regurgitator swam back and forth, transporting crates of shoes into the windmill; they wouldn't have their soles dampened.

Ernest Tremor's soles were saturated. He meticulously wiped his feet outside Chatter and Banter's door before knocking. The startled geese put their telescope away and waddled haughtily towards the door.

'What do you want?' Chatter eyed the small man who was already trembling.

'E-Ernest Tr-Tremor, Natural Disaster Expert. Do you have any tea?'

Chatter's harsh features softened. The man was admitted.

'You study these *disasters*?' Chatter scrutinised him over her teacup.

Ernest nodded, trembling.

'Work must be slow,' Banter commented sympathetically.

Ernest coloured.

'You're wasting your time here, dear, there isn't a quieter village!' Banter continued.

There was a clap of thunder. Suddenly, the man ceased to tremble and set down his teacup defiantly.

'Ladies, please! Have some dignity. The Earth is crumbling around you, for goodness sake! Do something to help yourselves and those around you! What are you afraid of?

Losing the old Arbsitchy and the structure of things? Frightened of change? Face up to your fear! If you are to remain figures of respect, you have to move with the times and adapt. Thanks for the tea, by the way.' He tipped his hat before diving into the water.

The geese opened their beaks in protest, but no sound emerged. After a few minutes they rose solemnly and followed the small man into the water.

'How can someone that small have so much to say?'

'I couldn't get a word in edgeways.'

The geese waddled up the hill with their necks held high and their beaks in the air. Mr Tremor sniffed the air and scoured the heavens, looking for a flicker of humanity in Weather's stony visage. As the geese approached, the sky roared as though it would rip in two.

'Found you,' Ernest breathed. He tipped his hat in the direction of the roar. Weather blew it off in response.

Inside the windmill, there was a loud vibration. Stiletta banged on the wall in annoyance.

'Sorry!' the draughty Draftness replied, 'I'm a bit nervous.'

Chatter and Banter donned their gas masks left over from the War.

On seeing what he thought was fear in the eyes of the geese — or perhaps their eyes watered from the windmill's stench — Cromdork and the Regurgitator touched each goose's shoulder and chorused, 'We told you so!'

'I *beg* your pardon?' Banter said, ruffled.

'If this isn't freak weather, I don't know what is!' Cromdork cried excitedly.

Terrified, Furnace darted out of the restaurant. Ernest noticed the sky darken and heard it growl.

'He's the problem, isn't he?'

'What do you mean?' Furnace bellowed.

Mr. Tremor ignored him. He addressed Weather, whispering, 'You could do so much better, you know. You want someone who'll accept you as you are and not try to change you. Everyone has cloudy days or feels a little overcast at times, but right now —'

Ernest was interrupted by an ear-splitting crack; a tornado spiralled from the sky, circling the chef, who ran around like a headless chicken. Ernest raised an eyebrow at Weather, smiling. The tornado reluctantly burnt itself out, causing the freed Furnace to drop his meat cleaver and flee in a cowardly manner.

'You're behaving like a spoilt child and your behaviour is endangering others!' Ernest cried, gesturing towards the villagers huddled inside the windmill. 'Tying yourself in knots over some strutting cockerel!'

The sky lightened and a gentle rain ensued, refreshing the earth. The sun peeked out shyly from behind its cloudy shroud.

'Don't be afraid,' Ernest said calmly.

Weather noticed that this man had a quiet power. She felt sad that he would be leaving soon, now that she was calm. She attempted to re-summon her anger to keep him in the village longer, but she was exhausted.

'There's no point trying that. Besides, I like to keep a memento from each disastrous scene I come across...'

'That's so sweet!' Stiletta cried.

'What?' Cromdork and the windmill chorused.

'He wants her to be his memento!' the Regurgitator announced. The rat really was getting good at his craft; he'd heard Stiletta's thoughts before she'd vocalised them.

'Weather, I'd like to take care of you, not change you, but spend the rest of my days trying to figure you out. Will you marry me?' Ernest asked earnestly.

Everyone, including The Royal Draftness, was silent. Stiletta clutched her lucky sandal strap. Weather's response was a rainbow in the shape of the letter Y. It truly was the calm after the storm.

***

Of course, it took a while for the village to recover from Weather's destruction, and even longer for Chatter and Banter to get over feeling hurt; even now, they're only coldly polite towards Cromdork.

Weather felt her anger towards Furnace rise up from time to time, but Ernest soon calmed her down whenever this happened.

Cromdork balanced his love of science with his new-found toleration of people — he was still working on his attitude towards women.

Stiletta's shoes survived the storm and I'm pleased to say that she has her very own shoe gallery in addition to her shop.

The Royal Draftness took over the post of village landmark. Chatter and Banter found it difficult to adjust to having a flatulent windmill as the village symbol.

Mr J. Long Flagpole retired from his position to be closer to his wife after their separation during the storm. However, he continued to wave Arbsitchy's flag during festivals.

Edmund the Evaluator and the Regurgitator became close friends; the rat liked to tell things and the tie-wearing troll enjoyed evaluating them.

And Furnace? He lies awake at night with his meat cleaver, compliment sheets and a bottle of vodka on his bedside table, and sleeps only when there is a thick mist and a light breeze. The villagers now neither deny their feelings nor let them dominate them as Weather had done and Furnace continues to do. Instead, they kept a balance between the two.

Lastly, the Regurgitator made it his life's work to pass on the chronicles of Sharson, the very same chronicles that you've just read.

Author Profile

Beth studied English Literature and Creative Writing at Lancaster University. She grew up in the countryside, surrounded by a menagerie of ducks, chickens, rabbits and guinea-pigs and her rural Rutland roots continue to inspire her writing. In addition to her writing, Beth is a performance poet who has enjoyed success in national competitions and festivals. In 2012, she was a runner up in the Thynks Publications Poetry Competition and was a finalist in the 2009 Young Writers' Poetry Rivals Competition. Beth enjoys playing the harp, drinking tea and dancing in public places. She is not afraid of spiders.

Author of:

Buttercup and Her Many-Legged Friends

The Sharson Chronicles

Publisher Information

Rowanvale Books provides publishing services to independent authors, writers and poets all over the globe. We deliver a personal, honest and efficient service that allows authors to see their work published, while remaining in control of the process and retaining their creativity. By making publishing services available to authors in a cost-effective and ethical way, we at Rowanvale Books hope to ensure that the local, national and international community benefits from a steady stream of good quality literature.

For more information about us, our authors or our publications, please get in touch.

www.rowanvalebooks.com
info@rowanvalebooks.com